A VISCOUNT FOR CHRISTMAS

CHRISTMAS SCANDALS
BOOK ONE

SUZANNA MEDEIROS

A VISCOUNT FOR CHRISTMAS

An unexpected Christmas gift…

When Viscount Isaac Thornton returns home for his mother's annual Christmas gathering, the last thing he expects to find is a beautiful woman sleeping in his bed. But Celia isn't yet another woman trying to trap him into marriage. She's his younger sister's best friend and now she's all grown up.

Celia Rowland outgrew the infatuation she had for Thornton years ago. When a misunderstanding means she's been compromised, her mother insists they get married.

One house party and two people trying to escape a forced wedding who just might get the Christmas gift they didn't know they wanted.

A VISCOUNT FOR CHRISTMAS was previously released in the multi-author anthology

Christmas Kisses. It is a Regency Historical Romance and contains the following themes: compromised heroine, scandal, best friend's brother, stranger in his bed, house party.

To learn about Suzanna Medeiros's future books, you can sign up for her newsletter at https://www.suzannamedeiros.com/newsletter.

"Am I making you uncomfortable?"

She was silent for a moment, and he feared the worst. He was about to release her hand when she shook her head. "No."

"So you don't mind it when I hold your hand like this? When I kiss your wrist?"

He repeated the movement, and this time her slightly dazed expression was his reward.

"No."

His grip tightened on her hand. "I'd like to kiss you, Celia. May I?"

Her nod was immediate.

He leaned closer, stopping when their faces were only inches apart. "Are you certain you don't mind?"

"Thornton…"

The pleading note in her voice told him clearly that she wanted this as much as he did. He closed the distance between them, pleased when she met him halfway.

He meant to keep the kiss light, not wanting to scare her away. But then she made a soft sound of pleasure, and all his good intentions flew out the window.

The only parts of them that touched were their hands and lips, but he did deepen the kiss. When his tongue touched her bottom lip, she sighed and opened her mouth to accept him.

His skin was on fire, his need for this woman growing with every second that passed as their mouths moved together as if they had done this a thousand times before. She leaned in closer, and her other hand went to his shoulder, but still he resisted the overwhelming need to pull her close.

The sudden jolt of the carriage coming to a halt brought an end to their kiss. He pulled back, as did she. Their gazes locked for several long moments.

He still held one of her hands, and her other hand rested on his shoulder.

"Celia—"

The rattle of the carriage door handle had him releasing her and moving away to preserve Celia's modesty.

In these very difficult times, I hope we can all manage to find a little joy.

- Suzanna -

CHAPTER 1

December 1816

IT WAS PAST MIDNIGHT when Viscount Isaac Thornton reached his estate in Surrey. He'd been on horseback for several hours. Normally the ride wasn't a difficult one, but with the cold temperatures, he'd needed to stop frequently to change horses.

Filled with a bone-deep fatigue that emphasized the unwelcome fact he'd recently passed his thirtieth birthday, all he wanted to do was sleep. He wasn't looking forward to the next week. His mother's yearly Christmas party would be yet another opportunity for her to remind him he needed to settle down and produce an heir. He couldn't avoid his mother's matchmaking altogether, but he could limit the duration of his suffering. Which was why he'd originally planned to arrive the day before Christmas and depart again the day after the holiday.

She'd successfully thwarted those plans with the greatest weapon in her arsenal—guilt. He'd received her letter that afternoon. In it, she told him how much she looked forward to spending quality time with him. She'd gone on to inform him that his two younger sisters, who lived in the north of England, wouldn't be attending because the roads were impassable after a heavy snowfall that hadn't reached Surrey. To alleviate what he knew would be her very real disappointment, he'd changed his plans and set out to join her when her house party would still be in full swing.

If he were being honest with himself, London had become tedious of late, especially after his friends and most of his acquaintances quit town and headed to their own estates for the holiday season. His mother's letter was a convenient excuse to return home earlier than planned.

He apologized to the sleepy groom who greeted him moments after he reached the stables. He was relieved to discover the manor was quiet as he made his way to the front door on foot. Perhaps his mother hadn't invited that many people this year.

But even as the thought occurred to him, he knew it was a futile wish. Christmas was his mother's favorite time of the year, and she was known for her winter house parties. This year wouldn't be any different.

He was surprised when the front door was opened by Saunders, their butler, and not a footman. He'd hoped to surprise his mother, but apparently she knew him too well. She'd expected him to set out for Surrey after receiving her letter.

He greeted the older man and handed him his hat and greatcoat, barely taking in the evergreen boughs and festive decorations that tastefully highlighted the fact the festive season was upon them. He'd started toward the stairs when Saunders coughed discreetly.

Thornton turned to face him.

"Your mother wishes to speak with you, my lord."

Thornton frowned. No doubt she wanted to tell him who she'd invited and why he should pay particular attention to each one of them. He'd just arrived, and already the matchmaking had begun.

He nodded. "I'll speak to her in the morning."

"She insisted—"

Thornton wouldn't take his annoyance out on this man whom he'd known since he was a child. Saunders was merely carrying out Lady Thornton's instructions.

"I already know what she wants to speak to me about."

"But—"

"Good night, Saunders. I'll speak to my mother first thing in the morning. And get some rest yourself." The man had no doubt been awake since dawn.

Before Saunders could say another word, Thornton turned and made his way upstairs.

He didn't ring for his valet when he reached his bedroom, too tired to care about the lecture the man would deliver tomorrow as he tossed his clothes onto a chair.

It was dark, but he didn't need to light a candle. He made his way to the bed and slid under the covers. His eyes were closing when a small movement on the other side of the bed chased away his fatigue.

He was imagining things. Or, more likely, he'd already fallen asleep and was dreaming. Still, he was wide awake now. He rolled over and narrowed his gaze on the other side of the bed, where he could see a small bundle wrapped in his blankets.

In retrospect, he should have sprung from the bed and thrown on his clothes. But he didn't really expect to find anything, and so he pulled back the bedsheets. It took his befuddled senses several seconds to process the fact he wasn't alone.

Someone was already asleep in his bed—a woman, to be precise. She lay with her back to him, and he could only stare at her for what felt like the longest minute of his life.

His fumbling in the dark hadn't caused her to move, so she must be asleep. His gaze took in the long golden hair that covered most of her back. Unbound, which surprised him. Unable to stop himself, he gazed down to where her hair ended just above the curve of her hip, which was covered in a white nightgown. The blankets covered the rest of her, and he resisted the temptation to drag them down even farther.

Casting aside the temptation to see whether she would be well endowed, he shifted onto his back and slung a hand over his eyes. He doubted very much that his mother had arranged this woman as a welcome-home present for him. She'd probably wanted to warn him that she had given away his room to another guest.

Which meant he had to dress again and find a servant to lead him to a room that was unoccupied.

He rose to a seating position with a muffled groan. He thought he'd been quiet, but the shifting of his weight must have woken the woman, because she rolled onto her back. Her eyes blinked open, and she let out a sleepy yawn. And then a scream.

That should have had him moving with alacrity, gathering up his clothes and escaping into the dressing room. But his brief glimpse at her form before she'd pulled up the bedcovers caused him to freeze. In the dim light, he could see that she was, indeed, well endowed.

Why did these things never happen to him under better circumstances? For it was clear now that he wasn't dreaming. If he were, she would have beckoned him to her with open arms. Instead, the woman in his bed had gathered up the blankets and held them to her breast like a shield.

"What are you doing here? You must leave at once!"

Yes, this wasn't a dream. "This is my bedroom."

Her mouth gaped open before she closed it with a snap. "You're not suggesting…" She took a deep breath and began again. "We can sort out this mess tomorrow morning. But a gentleman would leave without question and find another bedroom."

He couldn't resist teasing her. "Perhaps I'm not a gentleman."

She sputtered, speechless. Taking pity on her, he slipped from the bed with a soft curse.

"I don't know why you're upset. I'm the injured party here."

Something about the prim tone of her voice seemed familiar. He strode to the window and drew back the curtains to let in some of the moonlight. Then he returned to the bed—the side the woman occupied—and leaned forward to examine her. She leaned back with a squawk.

His eyes roamed over her face. Blond hair, blue eyes... she could have been anyone. But then he saw the small mole at the corner of her right eye.

"Celia Rowland?"

She huffed out an impatient breath. "That's Miss Rowland to you, my lord. Now will you please leave?"

He had to give her credit. Another woman might have given in to a fit of vapors at finding a man in her bed, but not Celia. He remembered her only as his youngest sister's friend. She'd been pretty, and he remembered finding her sweet, but she'd also been much too young for him the last time he'd seen her. He couldn't deny that she'd grown into a beautiful young woman.

He didn't miss the way her gaze dipped to his bare chest and couldn't hold back his smirk. "Like what you see?"

Her eyes met his again. "I was merely—"

"Admiring my fine form? Wondering if you'd asked me to leave too soon?"

She let out an impatient huff. "Is it your intention to compromise me?"

And that's when the reality of the situation settled into place. His understanding came too late, however, because the bedroom door was thrown open.

CHAPTER 2

THE DOWAGER VISCOUNTESS THORNTON had shown Celia to her son's room a few hours earlier, telling her that something was amiss with the room she was supposed to occupy. She'd assured Celia that he wasn't expected back that night, so it had come as a shock to find herself sharing a bed with the almost-naked viscount.

The man for whom she'd had a *tendre* when she was still a silly young girl who only interacted with him on rare occasions when she was visiting his sisters. Despite his well-known penchant for teasing, she knew Thornton would never harm her. He would dress and then find somewhere else to sleep that night.

But even more shocking than her unexpected awakening was the sound of the bedroom door being thrown open with such force it bounced off the wall with a loud boom. And of course the person standing in the doorway would be her mother. How did she even know Celia had switched rooms for the night? Mama had already retired when Thornton's mother escorted her to this room.

Her mother held an oil lamp aloft as she stepped into the room, her eyes and mouth open in outrage. But then her mouth snapped close, and the glint in her eye made it clear she was delighted to catch them in such a compromising position. Celia in her nightgown, clutching a blanket to her breast, and Thornton standing in only his smallclothes, uncaring that his chest was bare.

Heavens, what a chest it was. He'd caught her staring, but could he blame her?

"What is the meaning of this?"

Celia wanted to roll her eyes at her mother's theatrics, but the situation was dire. "Nothing happened, Mama. It was a misunderstanding."

Thornton ignored her mother's theatrics. Instead, he walked over to the clothing he'd deposited on a chair, acting for all the world as though he were fully dressed, and collected the garments.

"If you'll excuse me for a moment," he said to her mother with a small bow. He moved off to the dressing room, closing the door behind him.

Her mother, however, seemed content to wake the entire house. Celia rose from the bed, hoping to drag her mother into the bedroom and close the door.

She was too late. She'd only managed to take a step in her mother's direction when others began to move into place behind her mother. She reached for her dressing gown, donning it with haste, as guests began doing everything in their power to peer over her mother's shoulders.

"Mama—"

"This is enough. There is nothing to see here. Please go to bed."

The dowager viscountess pushed her way past the growing crowd. Celia's mother resisted but finally allowed Lady Thornton to drag her into the bedroom and close the door behind her. Murmured voices of protest could be heard, dimming after a minute had passed. Celia had no doubt that an army of footmen was leading the guests back to their rooms. They never would have left otherwise.

Lady Thornton frowned at Celia's mother. "For heaven's sake, please lower your voice." She turned to Celia. "Can you explain what is happening here and why your mother sought to raise the entire household?"

Thornton chose that moment to step out of the dressing room. He didn't have to say a word. The rumpled state of his clothing told his mother everything.

"I demand that you repair the damage you've done to my daughter's good name." Mama was almost screeching.

"Damage that wouldn't have been done if you'd kept your voice down," Lady Thornton said.

Mrs. Rowland waved her finger in their hostess's face. "I am not content to sweep this matter under the rug and act as though your son hasn't defiled my daughter!"

If there was one thing Celia's mother was good at, it was putting on a show. Even though most of her audience had been forcibly removed, it was clear she wasn't about to quit the stage.

"Nothing happened, Mama. His Lordship didn't know I was here. He'd just discovered my presence and was about to leave."

She caught the look that Lady Thornton cast toward her son and braved a quick glance at the viscount before looking away again. All she could think about was the muscles she'd seen in that all-too-short glance. But it had been enough to make it clear that this man did not need to pad his clothing. Nor did he need to wear constrictive garments to hold in his waistline as her father had done when he was alive.

"I regret that you had to find out about my betrothal to Miss Rowland in this manner. We'd planned to keep it a secret for a little while longer."

She could only stare at Thornton in disbelief. She almost thought she'd misheard him until her mother let out a disgruntled snort.

"You will make an announcement tomorrow. We can't have people gossiping about my daughter."

Thornton nodded once.

"This isn't necessary—" Celia began.

Mama cut off her protest. "I'd expected better behavior from you." Her frown was almost laughable. Celia had no doubt that her mother was delighted, and everyone in the room knew it.

"Mama—"

"You'll be married soon. Before Christmas."

If the viscount was angry, he hid it well. "Before the beginning of the new year."

Her mother was going to argue, but Lady Thornton spoke first. "Of course. We'll need time to prepare and to send out the announcements. And a special license will need to be procured."

That seemed to mollify her mother. Having trapped one of the wealthiest men in England into marrying her daughter, she'd want everyone to know about it.

Thornton turned his back on their mothers and gave her a bow. When he spoke, his voice was low, for her ears only. "We'll find a way out of this. You won't be forced into a marriage you don't want."

She searched his blue eyes for a hint of anger. He must think she'd planned this, and that thought caused her a pang of dismay. "Nor you."

With a nod, he turned to leave the room. He extended his arm to his mother, who took it with aplomb.

Her mother waited just long enough for the door to close behind the pair before allowing a grin to spread across her face. She rushed to Celia and took hold of her hands.

"That was well done! I never expected this from

you. Placing yourself in the viscount's bed was a stroke of genius."

She tried to hold on to her composure as her mother clapped her hands together in glee.

"I must admit I was surprised when Lady Thornton came to collect you this evening. But now I see she had the same intention as I did."

Shock went through her. "You don't think… Did the two of you plan this together?"

Her mother waved a hand in dismissal. "No, of course not. But I did follow to see where you were going. When I realized she was bringing you here, I decided to wait to see what would happen. I was just about to retire when the viscount arrived."

She couldn't have heard correctly. "You knew this was going to happen? You saw the viscount enter the room and didn't stop him?"

Her mother's eyes narrowed. "Of course not. Who am I to thwart fate?"

"Fate? Mama, we can't trap the viscount into marrying me."

"It doesn't matter now. A fair number of people saw you in the viscount's bedroom. And when they discover he has arrived…" She raised one shoulder in a casual shrug.

"He can leave again before anyone learns of his

arrival. No one needs to know why you were so upset tonight."

She started for the door, intending to go after the viscount and Lady Thornton, but was pulled up short by her mother.

"You will do no such thing. For the first time in your life, you have finally done something right when it comes to your search for a husband, and I will not allow you to ruin it."

"We can't do this. It isn't right."

Her mother's gaze hardened on hers. "You've been reading too many stories about romantic love. It's about time you learn that such notions are fit only for fairy tales. Yours will be a marriage to be envied."

Her mother made her way to the door. Celia's hopes of leaving to find Thornton were dashed with her parting words. "I have no qualms about explaining why I was so upset. There will be no hiding what happened here tonight. Congratulate yourself, my dear. You are about to become the new Viscountess Thornton."

With that, her mother strode from the room, a satisfied smile on her face.

Celia collapsed onto the bed and stared up at

the ceiling as her thoughts whirled. She knew her mother well enough to guarantee she would not willingly veer from this course. She only hoped the viscount would be able to devise a way out of this mess.

CHAPTER 3

ONE OF THE SERVANTS would escort Thornton to a bedroom that wasn't occupied, but first he needed to speak to his mother in private. He struggled to rein in his temper as he escorted her to her bedroom, refusing to give their guests another reason to gawk.

He vowed that he wouldn't yell as she opened her bedroom door and moved to the side to allow him to enter. He barely took in the surroundings of the pale yellow and lavender room, which hadn't changed since he was a young boy. He'd always enjoyed coming to visit his mother here, but now he could feel the control he held over his anger starting to come undone.

Celia Rowland wouldn't have been in his

bedroom if his mother hadn't arranged for her to sleep there. If she were any other woman who'd wanted to take advantage of the situation to trap him into marriage, she wouldn't have been so surprised by his presence. There was none of the archness he knew women displayed when they were playing a role, and he could tell her concern was genuine despite the moment of awareness that had passed between them when she'd stared at his body. If she'd meant to trap him, she would have gone out of her way to ensure she was well and truly compromised, but instead she'd wanted him to leave as soon as possible.

He ignored the little niggle of disappointment that he hadn't even gotten to kiss her before all hell had broken loose.

Somehow, he managed to keep his voice even when he faced his mother. "Were you really that desperate to have me wed that you would stage what just happened?"

She drew an audible breath and glared at him. He'd expected all manner of excuses from her, but not anger.

"Me? Why didn't you heed Saunders's warning? I don't know what type of adventures you get up to when you're in town, nor do I want to know, but

Celia is a gently bred young woman. To think that my own son would try to take advantage of her."

His indignation evaporated in the face of her own. "I didn't know she'd be there."

His mother's anger didn't abate with his protest of innocence. "Saunders has never been derelict in his duties and you'll never convince me otherwise."

He crossed to the small sitting area set up on one side of the large chamber and dropped onto the chaise longue.

"I was tired. He informed me you wanted to see me right away, but I told him I already knew what you wanted to speak to me about. He protested, but I insisted. He must have assumed you told me about Celia in the letter you'd sent." A part of him still couldn't believe that his mother was entirely innocent when it came to the fiasco that had taken place that night. "Why would you put her in my room? Surely you haven't invited so many people that we've run out of bedrooms?"

His mother sat next to him on the opulent lavender seat, her shoulders drooping. "I put her next to her mother. But I came upon Mrs. Rowland speaking to Lord Gravenhurst and could scarce believe what I was hearing. He was going to compromise her so she would be forced to marry him." She met Thornton's gaze. "I couldn't allow that to happen. Mrs. Rowland hasn't made her frustration a secret. She's arranged for all manner of suitors, but her daughter didn't accept any of them. Still, I couldn't allow Celia's hand to be forced in that manner.

The irony of the situation wasn't lost on him. "And instead, I compromised her."

"I didn't want this to happen. But you should know that Celia is a good match for you."

"It appears that everyone will get what they want except for Celia and me."

"And the odious Lord Gravenhurst. Oh, why did I invite him?"

He placed a hand over his mother's and squeezed it lightly. "Because he was a friend of the family."

She shook her head. "Not really. Your father didn't like him, but for some reason he felt it important to cultivate the man's friendship. He has power in parliament."

"Power that is waning."

His mother met his gaze and frowned. "Truly? So I kept up the acquaintance for no reason?"

He gave his mother's hand one last squeeze before releasing it. "How could you know?"

No, his mother wouldn't have heard the whispers that were spoken about the man. He'd buried two wives, and now his eyes were set on Celia Rowland. No matter what came out of tonight's events, he couldn't be sorry that she'd escaped the man's clutches.

He rose and stared down at his mother where she remained seated. She seemed so small, and her distress was genuine.

"Everything will be fine. I'll speak to Miss Rowland tomorrow, and we'll decide how to proceed."

"Do you think she'll end the betrothal before it's even been announced? I fear what her mother would do in that situation."

He bent and dropped a kiss on his mother's forehead. "Try to get some sleep. We'll sort things out tomorrow."

He wasn't surprised to find Saunders waiting for him outside his mother's bedroom. To his credit, the butler didn't betray a hint of censure and led him, in silence, to another bedroom.

Despite his parting words to his mother, Thornton didn't think he'd be able to sleep a wink that night. All signs of the fatigue that had led him to behave so carelessly had fled.

IT WAS IMPOSSIBLE TO IGNORE THE WHISPERS THE next morning when he made his way to the breakfast room. He'd finally managed to find solace from his spinning thoughts in sleep, but he was awake far too early for his liking.

His gaze swept over the many guests, far more than usual. Did his mother invite everyone in the county? It would figure that she would be hosting her largest Christmas gathering the year he committed such a faux pas as unintentionally compromising a young woman.

He called out greetings to everyone as he crossed the room to the sideboard. He didn't see Celia, but he did spy Baron Gravenhurst.

After piling up his plate, he made his way to the empty seat next to the man. His mother's revelation that Celia's mother had entered into an agreement with the baron to have him compromise—if not outright defile—her daughter angered him. He hoped his mother had been mistaken in what she'd overheard.

It didn't take him long to discover that wasn't the case.

Gravenhurst glared at him, not bothering to

hide his displeasure as Thornton took his seat. "I didn't know I would have a rival for Miss Rowland's affections."

Thornton met and held the man's gaze. "Miss Rowland and I have known each other for some time. She was a good friend to one of my sisters."

He let out an unseemly snort. "And was she also a special friend to you?"

"The last time I saw her, she was little more than a child. I don't make it a habit of robbing the cradle for female companionship." Unlike some people, he added mentally. Both the baron's wives had been young, just out in society. It rankled that this man, who was old enough to be Celia's father, had thought to coerce her into marrying him.

Gravenhurst merely shrugged and turned his attention back to his plate. "I can't say I blame you. I've never been good at waiting for the wedding night myself."

Thornton's fingers tightened on his fork. Regretting his decision to sit next to this man, he forced a mouthful of eggs down his dry throat. Maybe if he ignored the baron, he would stop talking.

But it was almost impossible to ignore the fact Celia had experienced a near miss last night. If not for his mother's quick thinking in seeing her out of harm's way, she could very well have found herself betrothed to this loathsome man this morning. He didn't want to contemplate such a fate befalling sweet, luscious Celia.

Gravenhurst leaned closer to him. "Of course, if you change your mind, I will have no problem taking her off your hands. I don't even care about her ruined reputation," he said with a wink.

Thornton's fork clattered onto his plate, but the baron was oblivious to his growing anger.

"Young man like yourself, you don't want to tie yourself down too quickly. Say the word, and she can be Lady Gravenhurst."

Over his dead body. Thornton met the baron's gaze, allowing ice to touch his words. "I don't know what you think happened last night, but you should stop talking right now. The next time you address me, I would advise you to remember that Miss Rowland is under my protection. I would have no qualms about calling you out."

He almost wanted Gravenhurst to defy his warning. Then he could plow his fist through the man's face.

CHAPTER 4

C ELIA NEVER WANTED to leave this room again, but she knew her mother would never allow her the luxury of privacy. When a maid arrived with one of her outfits, Celia sighed and began preparations for the day.

It didn't matter that no one had seen the viscount last night. Many had seen her in his bedroom, and when they realized he was in residence… She shuddered at the thought that everyone would be talking about them. Gossiping and jumping to all manner of incorrect assumptions.

Assumptions that her mother would do everything in her power to encourage.

When the maid finished putting up Celia's hair,

she stood and braced herself for the day. But how did one prepare themselves to be at the center of a scandal? She knew many young women who would thrive under the speculation she was about to face —she'd met many of them during her last season. But she'd always had to be dragged out of her preferred hiding spot sitting on the outskirts of the many ballrooms she'd frequented.

For a fleeting moment, she thought she might be able to dart downstairs quickly, grab something to eat, and then retreat somewhere quiet where she could hide for the rest of the day. But when the maid opened the door to leave, her mother brushed past the young woman.

"Oh good. I thought for sure you were going to try to hide today."

And there went all thought of trying to find a reprieve. Celia knew this house much better than her mother, after all, since she'd stayed here several times when she was younger. She had no doubt she'd be able to find somewhere to conceal herself from everyone who would be speculating about what had happened last night.

She sighed as her mother tucked Celia's arm into her own and all but dragged her from the viscount's bedroom. To everyone who saw them, it would look like a show of support. But her mother grasped her arm a little too tightly, and Celia knew there would be no escaping her.

Walking into the breakfast room was worse than she'd imagined. The soft hum of conversation came to an abrupt halt, and every eye in the room turned to look at her. There must be at least twenty people present. If her mother didn't have such a tight grip on her arm, she would have turned around and walked back out.

Lady Thornton came to her rescue, crossing to her side and almost prying her from her mother's grasp. Together they walked over to the sideboard, the sound of whispers resuming as they passed. Mama followed closely, as though afraid Celia would somehow escape.

"I hope you had a restful sleep after last night's interruption. I should have told your mother that I'd temporarily moved you because your room wasn't ready. I never thought she would become so worried when she couldn't find you."

Celia didn't miss her mother's indrawn breath behind her, and she braced herself for a scene.

"I'm just glad Saunders was able to warn my son about the temporary change of rooms when he arrived early this morning."

Celia loved this woman. The whispers increased behind them, the dowager viscountess's words passing from person to person. With any luck, this would be the end of any discussion about forcing her and Thornton into a marriage.

"And where is Lord Thornton this morning?" Her mother's voice, much louder than necessary, set Celia's nerves on edge. She wasn't going to let this go. "Oh, there he is, sitting next to Lord Gravenhurst."

She caught the tense expression on Lady Thornton's face and the way the dowager viscountess's mouth tightened at her mother's mention of the baron. Celia couldn't help feeling as though she were missing something important and would have to ask Thornton about that later.

But at least the dowager viscountess had paved the way forward. If no one knew about the viscount accidentally getting into bed with her, they could still end the betrothal without any scandal. Perhaps at the end of the house party, when everyone left to return to their own homes in time for Christmas day, they could finally put an end to this nonsense.

Almost as though she'd summoned him, Thornton joined them. He invited them to join him at the end of the table, which was mostly unoccupied.

Lady Thornton led most of the conversation, trying to steer it away from Celia and Thornton. Celia noticed the displeasure on her mother's face and knew the morning's reprieve wouldn't last long. She'd demand a formal announcement be made in front of their guests or expose what had really happened last night.

Celia chanced a glance at Thornton, taking in his expression as he spoke to her three cousins who had moved down the table to join them. Lily, Iris and Violet. They would accost her or their aunt the moment breakfast was over. She dreaded to think what Mama would tell them about last night's happenings.

As though sensing her gaze, Thornton turned to look at her. His smile betrayed no anger at the situation in which they found themselves. It wasn't difficult to smile back at him.

Thornton sought the reprieve of his study after breakfast.

His mother's statements had quieted the speculation about what had happened last night, but they all knew Mrs. Rowland wouldn't be content to let the matter rest. He would have to make the announcement about their betrothal later that evening or risk her telling everyone she'd found them alone together in his bedroom.

To say he was annoyed with the woman would be a vast understatement, but at least she'd given up her scheme to create a match between her daughter and Gravenhurst. If his announcement kept that from happening, then he couldn't be sorry about putting off Saunders's attempts to warn him.

He didn't have any work to do, but that didn't stop his annoyance when a knock sounded at the door.

Instead of calling out for the intruder to enter, he rose from his desk and strode to the door. If this was Gravenhurst, back to make lewd comments about Celia, he'd have no qualms about doing whatever was necessary to shut the man's mouth.

His anger returning to the surface, he swung open the door. He deflated when he saw Saunders standing in the hallway.

The butler raised a brow at Thornton's abrupt behavior, but he didn't comment on it. "Your mother has asked to see you in her sitting room."

Thornton blew out a breath. "Of course."

He wondered what more she would have to say to him, but at this point he would not ignore another of her summonses.

The door to the sitting room was closed. Normally his mother kept it open, but like him, she probably wanted a moment of calm away from their guests.

He didn't knock, letting himself into the room and moving to close the door behind him before he realized that his mother wasn't there. Instead, Celia waited by the window, gazing out onto the grounds. She turned and met his gaze.

He didn't close the distance between them, but he did take care to lock the door. The last thing they needed was another interruption.

"Your mother thought we should talk."

"By all means." He indicated she should sit in one of the chairs and then took his own seat in the chair that was next to hers at an angle.

He couldn't help but wonder what his mother meant to accomplish by arranging this secret meeting.

Celia sighed. "I need to apologize."

He raised one brow. "I was under the assumption you were as much a victim of your mother's matchmaking attempts as I."

"I have no idea what happened last night. Your mother assured me that you weren't expected but that if you did arrive home early, the staff were supposed to show you to another room."

"That was the plan. But I arrived late and brushed aside Saunders's insistence that I needed to speak to my mother. You know how that turned out."

Celia let out a sigh. "You're not to blame. I still don't know why your mother even insisted that I sleep in your bedchamber last night, but she was quite adamant that my room wouldn't do."

He watched her carefully, searching for even a hint she was lying to him. She wouldn't be the first woman to try to trap him into marriage by having him compromise her, after all. But he could detect nothing but honesty in her clear blue eyes. Her hands were clenched together in her lap, her knuckles almost white.

"I've tried to talk some sense into Mama, but she won't listen to me. I'm afraid she won't be dissuaded from this course of action." She shook her head, a small vee forming between her brows. "This behavior is most unlike her. She can't honestly believe that you and I…" She looked away, unable to complete that sentence. She took a deep breath and continued. "You shouldn't have to suffer for her overreach."

Her statement unsettled him. "Overreach is a harsh term, and unjust. You're a gently bred young woman, and your family lineage is impeccable. Wasn't your grandfather an earl?"

"Yes, but that doesn't mean I want to trap you into a marriage you don't want. Mama has been trying to find me a husband for some time, but I never thought she'd force a match."

He couldn't detect any sign that Celia was putting on a show for him. Still, he continued. "She did find us together, and neither one of us was fully clothed."

She blushed and looked away from him. He remembered again how she'd looked him over and knew she was thinking about that moment as well.

Finally, she met his gaze again. "I'm going to break the betrothal."

He could only stare at her, convinced that she was speaking the truth. This foolish, selfless woman would allow her own reputation to fall into ruins to ensure his happiness.

A stirring of emotion caught him off guard. It

was admiration. And along with that a pull that urged him to save her. But not because he was self-less. No, because it was her, Celia Rowland. And he didn't want to see her suffer.

"We shouldn't act too hastily. At the very least, we should wait until the rest of the guests depart in two days' time. We don't want your mother to share the real reason for our betrothal."

Celia shuddered. "Heaven forbid. Normally I'd say my mother would never do something like this, but she's being most insistent and I'm a little afraid that she might."

"So you'll wait?"

"Yes, but only until the other guests depart. I don't want this situation to get any worse than it already is."

He frowned, knowing that if his mother was to be believed, Mrs. Rowland had planned for a much worse scenario. And his mother had no reason to lie.

Clearly, he hadn't been able to hide the anger that threatened to erupt every time he thought of Gravenhurst's intentions toward Celia.

She narrowed her eyes and tilted her head to one side as though trying to read his mind. "There's something you're not telling me."

There was no point in hiding the truth from her. If her mother was willing to concoct such a horrible plan with Gravenhurst, it was best Celia was on her guard. He tried not to think about the fact he wouldn't be there to protect her the next time her mother tried something similar.

"I'm telling you this because you need to know so that you can safeguard yourself in the future."

Her eyes widened, but she waited for him to continue.

"I spoke to my mother last night. I was convinced at the time that she had planned what happened together with your mother."

She gasped. "Surely she didn't—"

"No. As she reminded me, Saunders tried to prevent me from heading to my bedroom without speaking to her first. But I was tired and convinced that whatever she wanted to tell me could wait until morning."

"She was going to warn you that she'd placed me in your bedchamber."

"Yes. And she was angry when she thought I was, in fact, trying to compromise you."

"I can imagine," she said with a wince.

"Once my own anger abated, I realized she had

done everything in her power to ensure I didn't… stumble upon you."

Their eyes met and held for a long moment before she blushed again and looked away. Neither one needed to say that he'd done much worse than just stumble upon her.

"You should know that your mother had hoped to force a match between you and Gravenhurst. She had planned to catch the two of you together and then demand that you wed."

She gasped, her mouth hanging open. "She wouldn't. She wasn't happy when I discouraged my suitors last season, but she never pressed me about it. Why would she do something like that?"

The thought of Celia having suitors disturbed him, but he pushed away his discomfort. He'd felt the same when his sisters were being courted. It was natural that he would also be protective of one of their friends.

"Mother overheard them planning. To protect you, she arranged to have you switch rooms so he couldn't carry out the scheme."

"And instead, only succeeded in ensnaring you in the tangled mess."

"I was angry, yes, but not any longer."

She searched his gaze, her furrowed brow telling him she didn't believe him.

"Celia," he said, leaning forward. "I would do anything to ensure you're not tied to that man. You deserve better."

She let out a soft sigh. "That may be true, but this is my problem, not yours. At the end of this gathering, I will give you your freedom. And since I am now of age, I will let Mama know that much as she might desire it, she can't force me to wed. Any future attempts on her part to force a match between me and another man of her choosing will only lead to my ruin. I will *not* be forced to wed."

He couldn't help but wonder why she seemed so vehement in her opposition to marriage. Was it that she wanted to choose her future husband herself, or was she opposed to the institution altogether?

Much as he wanted to, he wouldn't ask. "We have time. For now, our best course of action will be to announce our betrothal."

She winced but didn't disagree with him.

"We need to let your mother believe that her plan has worked so she won't tell anyone about our little misunderstanding last night. I am not just worried about myself. When we end this pretend engagement, I want your reputation to remain intact."

She smiled, but there was a sadness in her eyes that pulled at his heart.

"We'll find a way forward, Celia. One that will get you everything you want."

She looked away for a moment, swallowing visibly before replying. "Thank you for your concern."

She rose from her seat, and he followed suit. "You should leave first. When Saunders sees you, he'll fetch your mother. She'll escort me from her chambers so no one will know we were alone together."

He bowed and took his leave, but he didn't want to. He wanted to stay and try to reassure Celia that everything would work out well in the end. But how could he do that when, despite what he'd told Gravenhurst, it wasn't in his power to protect her?

You could marry her in earnest. You're attracted to her, and your friendship is a stronger foundation than many have when they wed.

He ignored the errant thought and strode from the room without glancing back.

CHAPTER 5

THE DAY HAD BEEN AS DIFFICULT as Celia imagined. Despite the activities Lady Thornton had arranged to entertain her guests throughout the day, Celia's thoughts didn't stray far from what would happen over dinner.

Celia still couldn't believe her mother was behaving in such a manner. Yes, Mama had made no secret about wanting to see her wed, but to try to force her hand?

Dinner was lively, conversation flowing freely around them as they enjoyed the venison. Celia began to hope they'd avoided the whole ordeal. Perhaps the viscount's mother had convinced Mama not to pursue her current course of action.

Mama had been quiet over dinner, and Lady

Thornton had been masterful in encouraging everyone to share their plans for Christmas. That was only four days from now, but everyone would leave to make their way home in two days. Celia had to make it through that time without giving away the fact that her nerves were completely frayed.

She stole yet another glance at the head of the table, where Thornton was speaking to one of the guests seated to his left, an older widow whose name Celia couldn't remember. When his gaze sought out hers, there was a steely determination in his eyes that made her realize her hopes had been in vain.

The viscount rose, and conversation stopped as everyone gave him their attention. Celia glanced at her mother and couldn't miss the satisfied smile on her face.

She looked at Thornton again, marveling at how he could appear so calm. "I would like to take this opportunity to thank you all for joining us this year. What would Christmas be, after all, without one of my mother's house parties?" He paused, waiting for the murmurs of assent to die down. "I also have an announcement to make."

Celia straightened and tried not to cringe. Soon enough, everyone would be looking at her.

The viscount's gaze moved over everyone seated around the table. She'd thought there were a lot of people present at breakfast this morning, but the number seated along the long dining table made that group seem small.

She wondered if the dowager viscountess's Christmas gatherings were normally this large. She'd never attended before, even when Thornton's sisters were younger and she'd been a frequent visitor to the house.

Of course, it was just her bad luck that the first time she and Mama attended disaster had struck.

She kept her attention on Thornton, trying not to fret about all the witnesses to his announcement. It was impossible to ignore just how handsome he was. Of course, now that she knew what he looked like underneath his formfitting waistcoat and broad-shouldered topcoat, it was difficult to forget.

She'd fancied Thornton when she was younger, but she'd assumed that was just a youthful infatuation. During those summer visits, he'd been the attractive, dark-haired older brother to Emily and Julia. He'd always been patient with his sisters and, by extension, her. But his behavior now only cemented her good opinion of him. Any other man would have been angry about the situation in which they now found themselves. She'd expected bitter accusations about her scheming, perhaps even some pouting.

She should have known Thornton wouldn't behave in such a manner. He'd risen to the occasion with grace and aplomb. Their conversation earlier that day had confirmed that he wasn't happy about the current turn of events, but looking at him now, as he prepared to announce their betrothal, she could see no indication he'd been forced into this.

When his gaze reached her, a smile spread across his face. Her heart began to race when he lifted his glass of wine in her direction.

"I am very happy to announce that Miss Celia Rowland has consented to be my wife and will be the next Viscountess Thornton."

The silence that settled over the room was almost deafening, and she could feel the weight of all those gazes as everyone turned to look at her. Steeling her resolve, she raised her own glass in reply. With a tilt of her head and a forced smile, she took a sip of her wine.

Thornton's eyes remained locked on hers over his glass as he did the same. She was aware of movement around her as the rest of the guests raised their own glasses to toast to their happiness.

Thornton took his seat again, and the footmen sprang into action, removing their plates and then serving dessert. Plum pudding and an assortment of biscuits and macaroons were set out.

Slowly conversation resumed, but it was impossible for Celia to ignore the speculative glances cast her way. Mama, of course, was thrilled with the course of events, beaming with maternal pride.

Celia took a bite of the pudding but conceded she wouldn't be finishing dessert. She'd eaten little and imagined she would be starving come midnight, but it was impossible to ignore the nerves fluttering in her belly.

She wasn't accustomed to being at the center of so much attention, something which always left her uneasy. But beyond that, she'd come to an unsettling discovery. In that moment, when her eyes had met Thornton's as he'd made his toast, she'd become aware of an uncomfortable truth.

She'd thought herself past the youthful infatuation she'd once had for this man, but now she knew that wasn't true. Because a large part of her had wanted to believe his words were spoken in earnest. That he was announcing their marriage because he cared for her, perhaps even loved her. It was silly, the stuff of girlish dreams, but it was also her unfortunate reality.

The *tendre* she'd held for him had somehow blossomed into love. Perhaps she'd always loved him, but now she was aware of him in a way her younger self never could have imagined.

And because she cared too much to force him into a marriage he didn't want, she would have to let him go.

WHEN DINNER WAS OVER, THE WOMEN PROCEEDED to the drawing room, leaving the men behind. There would only be a short interlude before the evening's entertainment began, but it gave many the opportunity to swarm around her and demand answers to their questions.

Chief among them were her cousins, Lily, Iris, and Violet, who demanded to know every detail of her and Thornton's courtship. Celia tried to put them off, telling everyone she'd known the viscount since she was young and that everything had changed recently when they met again after not seeing one another for years. It wasn't a lie, but it lacked the details everyone wanted.

Finally, Lady Thornton rose and led the group to the music room. Bows of greenery were draped over the backs of the chairs that had been arranged around a pianoforte.

Celia made her way to the table that had been set up at the far side of the room with a large bowl of wassail. She took a deep breath, inhaling the rich scent of apple cider, spices, and brandy. She had a weakness for the warm drink and smiled widely at the footman who handed her a cup.

Her mother had secured seats for them at the front, but Celia chose to follow her cousins, who sat closer to the middle of the room. She could feel her mother's glare as she walked away.

The sound of animated conversation swept over her as many of the women indicated their intention to showcase their talents. Celia was relieved she would finally be able to settle back and enjoy the evening, secure in the knowledge that everyone's attention would no longer be fixed on her.

Lily sat to one side of her, Iris and Violet on the other, and they continued peppering her with questions. Asking her to share further details of her and Thornton's courtship, wanting to know how the viscount proposed and whether the wedding date had been set. They were less than content with Celia's vague answers.

Loud voices drifting through the doorway told her the men were finally joining them. She turned her back to the door, not wanting to be caught staring.

Lily squeezed her arm and leaned in to whisper in her ear. "I must admit I'm a little jealous. The viscount is the most handsome man here."

Celia agreed wholeheartedly. He was the most intriguing man of her acquaintance, and she'd come to know a fair number of them over the past few years as her mother did everything in her power to procure a match for her.

"He's also the youngest man here," she said.

Lily shook her head, her blond curls dancing about her face. "Don't be coy. You must give us more details. I will expire from curiosity."

Celia raised her brows. "Perhaps later, when there aren't quite so many ears around us."

Iris and Violet almost bounced in their seats. "Don't even think about excluding us. We don't care that Lily is the oldest."

When the men entered and settled toward the back of the room, it took every ounce of willpower

Celia possessed not to turn around and look for Thornton. Under other circumstances, she wouldn't have hesitated to wave a greeting to him, but now that there was so much talk surrounding the two of them, she didn't dare.

The dowager viscountess settled behind the pianoforte, starting the evening off with a beautiful rendition of "The First Noel." Celia had always enjoyed Lady Thornton's singing, having heard it many times in the past. The dowager's voice was deeper than that of many women's, lending a rich quality to the song that matched her playing. Celia's own voice was a moderately high soprano, which was ordinary in her opinion.

Her applause was heartfelt when Lady Thornton came to the end of the song. Thornton's mother rose and swept into a deep curtsy. This was a woman who was confident in her abilities and who didn't mind the attention that came with performing. Unlike Celia, who enjoyed singing and playing only in private or before a small group of acquaintances.

Lady Thornton gazed out over the group. "I'd like to invite anyone who wishes to have a turn. Who will be first?"

To Celia's horror, her mother rose. Mama didn't sing, which could only mean…

"I think my daughter should go first, all things considered."

And just like that, the relative peace of the past few minutes evaporated as everyone turned to look at her. Celia's thoughts raced as she searched for a reason not to perform for so many people.

Mama didn't give her a chance to come up with an excuse. "As you can all see, my daughter is shy and will need some encouragement."

She was going to kill her mother. Why was she doing this to her?

The polite applause and cajoling that followed her mother's statement gave her no choice. Despite wanting nothing more than to flee from the room, Celia took a deep breath and stood. The encouragements stopped then, and it was impossible to ignore the whispers. Some were from disgruntled women who'd wanted to showcase their own talents, and one person wondered if Celia could even play.

She'd be able to play, but she couldn't guarantee her voice wouldn't falter.

It was clear that she wouldn't be able to avoid the coming humiliation, so she might as well get it over with as quickly as possible. She gathered her hands together at her waist to keep them from shaking and made her way to the front of the room.

If she didn't make eye contact with anyone while she played, perhaps she could pretend this was one of those times when she'd played for Thornton's family. He'd even been there on occasion.

She lowered herself onto the bench, smoothing out her skirts. Her hands weren't shaking, something for which she was grateful. She ignored the sheet music Lady Thornton had piled for the guests. There was one Christmas carol she knew by heart, and she didn't want to prolong this ordeal by shifting through the music to find a different song. Unfortunately, it was also a relatively long song.

With a deep breath, she placed her hands on the keys, trying to convince herself this would be like all those other times she had played in this very room. But it was impossible to ignore the whispers. She was going to embarrass herself.

Movement to her left had her turning to see who was approaching. She expected to see her mother, or perhaps Lady Thornton was planning to join her. She never expected to see the viscount. While he'd watched her and his sisters perform on several occasions many years ago, he'd never once joined them. Could he even sing? If not, they would both be making a spectacle of themselves.

But she couldn't ignore the warmth that kindled inside her at his willingness to come to her aid. Again.

He smiled at her, causing her heart to flutter, but this time it wasn't caused by nerves. He turned his back to their audience and spoke in a low voice, for her ears only. "You don't need to be nervous. I've heard you perform, and you are more than up to the task."

She wasn't sure that was true, but with him at her side, standing next to her, most of the people would be looking at him and not her.

She took another deep breath and started playing the opening strains of "The Twelve Days of Christmas." The first few keys were rough, but it didn't take her long to fall back into the rhythm of the song. She'd played this many times and didn't really have to think about what she was doing.

Singing was another matter entirely. When she opened her mouth to begin, nothing came out. Fortunately, Thornton didn't wait for her lead and his rich baritone filled the room. She joined him on the second line of the song and their voices weaved together through the lyrics, melding perfectly. No one would guess that they'd never sung together before that night.

Her attention drifted from the keyboard. At first she looked down, not to help her play but to allow herself to concentrate on the song and not on the people who were watching them. But before long, her gaze drifted to Thornton as she watched him sing as though he made a regular habit of performing for others.

She didn't even realize that the rest of the guests had joined in, singing along with them, until she reached the very end of the song and her fingers stilled on the keys.

She smiled at Thornton, wondering why she'd never heard him sing before tonight. She remembered his sisters trying to get him to join them, but he'd never agreed.

She'd completely forgotten the audience until they broke out in enthusiastic applause. She tore her gaze from Thornton's, feeling the heat in her cheeks as she rose. She dipped into a curtsy and then took his arm as he escorted her back to her seat.

When she passed her mother, the secretive smile on Mama's face told her that she'd noticed Celia's reaction to the man. Everyone else would see that moment as proof that she and Thornton cared for one another, but Mama knew the match wasn't genuine. And apparently she now knew that Celia still cared for him, as she had when she was younger.

Celia settled back into her seat, relieved that she hadn't embarrassed herself. A steady stream of women took their turn singing and playing for the others. She couldn't let her guard down completely as she feared her mother would volunteer her for another song, but Mama must have realized she'd barely escaped public humiliation. If it hadn't been for Thornton's assistance, that outcome would have been certain.

Finally, Lady Thornton stood and thanked everyone for their participation. Celia couldn't help but notice the significant look she cast at her son before announcing the next portion of the evening's entertainment.

CHAPTER 6

OF COURSE, THERE WAS DANCING. His mother's Christmas parties grew more elaborate every year, and this was one tradition she'd instituted two years ago.

He stood to one side, chatting with some of the men, many of whom wanted to know if there was a gaming room. He promised to check with his mother and, if she hadn't planned one, to rectify the oversight himself.

While the guests milled about, most of the chairs were swiftly removed from the room. A few were placed in small groupings along two of the walls for those who wanted to sit, and when that task was completed, one of the older footmen took his place at the pianoforte. He had performed this task every year since his mother discovered the man had a natural talent for playing. He would play soft music while the guests conversed with one another.

He approached his mother and pulled her aside. "You've set up the card room?"

His mother sighed. "Of course. This isn't the first party I've hosted." She placed a hand on his arm. "But you'll remain?"

Against his will, Thornton's gaze drifted to Gravenhurst, who was staring at Celia with a slight frown on his face. He didn't particularly want to dance, but he would stay to keep the baron in line.

He nodded before rejoining the other group. His mother always set up the tables in the billiard room, and he told them they could proceed there.

He was surprised that only a few men departed, the rest opting to stay with their wives. He could only attribute their behavior to the sentimentality surrounding the Christmas season.

The footman had started to play a light tune that served as background music for the clustered guests. He knew that, as in previous years, most of the dancing would be done by the married couples and the young women who threw themselves into dancing with one another. They'd never behave in such a manner in London, of course, but here in the country, emboldened by the spirits Cook had added to the wassail, they'd have no qualms about enjoying themselves.

He gazed across the room to where Celia was standing with her three cousins, imagining they'd all join in the festivities soon.

He frowned when he saw Gravenhurst approach the group and bow. The man wouldn't dare ask Celia to dance with him…

Celia's gaze swept across the room before finally settling on him for a moment. And in her eyes he could see a plea for assistance. Given that she now knew this man's intentions toward her were far from honorable, she wouldn't feel comfortable dancing with him.

But when she looked at the baron again, the corners of her mouth lifted in a stiff smile. Dammit. Of course, she was going to accept. She was too polite to refuse him outright.

He didn't even realize he'd started to move, but when Gravenhurst raised a hand for Celia to take, Thornton was already at their side.

"Miss Rowland," he said with a bow. "I hope you haven't forgotten that you've promised me this first dance?"

Celia's expression warmed, her smile no longer

forced. "I thought perhaps you'd want to join the men who departed for other entertainments."

"And miss the opportunity to dance with you? Never."

He didn't even glance at Gravenhurst as he led her to the middle of the room, where two lines of women were already forming. He would be the only man in the set, but he had two younger sisters, so it wouldn't be the first time he'd have to entertain a group of females on his own.

The music became livelier, and soon he and Celia were moving through the figures of the dance, coming together and then parting again. There was no opportunity to talk privately, so they kept their banter light, conscious of the fact that the other dancers would be able to catch snippets of their conversation.

He could barely take his eyes off Celia throughout, mesmerized by her laughter and the joy radiating from her. He wasn't aware he was focused so intently on her until one of her cousins—Iris?—sighed loudly and commented to her sister that the two of them made a good match.

He should have been annoyed at the observation, but for some reason he wasn't. And he realized it was because his feelings for this woman were becoming complicated.

He started that dance thinking only to protect her from Gravenhurst, but by the time they reached the end, he realized that he wanted to spend more time with her.

They moved off to the side when the set was over, but he didn't leave. One glance at Gravenhurst told him the man was waiting for Thornton to do so, and he wasn't about to leave Celia unprotected.

He expected her cousins to surround them but saw that they were taking up their positions for the next set. His mother was deep in conversation with hers, so they wouldn't be joining them. Not that he expected Mrs. Rowland to protect her from Gravenhurst. She'd failed in that task once already, so he wasn't about to give her another opportunity to do so again.

They found two chairs that were unoccupied and settled into them.

"I didn't know you could sing." Celia gave her head a small shake. "I was fully prepared to make a fool of myself, and then I feared we'd both suffer that fate together."

"You wound me with your lack of faith."

Thornton was aiming for mock outrage, but Celia only laughed at him.

"You can hardly blame me for thinking that. All those times your sisters and I gave our little performances you never once joined us. Why was that?"

"My mother."

She tilted her head to one side. "I seem to recall her trying to cajole you into joining us on more than one occasion. I believed that you refrained because you didn't want to embarrass yourself."

He could understand why she'd thought as much. "It's quite the opposite, I'm afraid. Mother used to show me off all the time when I was a child, insisting we sing together whenever possible. Especially during her Christmas parties, which she's been hosting for as long as I can remember. I grew to hate it. Then when my voice deepened..." He shrugged. "I told her I'd lost the talent."

Celia smiled in sympathy. "I wish my own mother could be so easily put off. Honestly, I don't know what she was thinking. She knows I hate performing in front of large groups of people."

"She wanted to show you off."

Her mouth twisted in displeasure. "I'm sure it was more that she wanted to gloat about our betrothal. As though everyone here wasn't already talking about it." She shook her head. "At any rate, thank you for coming to my rescue."

"It was no great sacrifice," he said, realizing that he meant the words.

"Indeed, I never would have imagined our voices would meld together so perfectly."

That wasn't all Thornton wanted to meld together.

He cleared his throat and looked away, trying to tame his wayward thoughts. His attraction to Celia was almost embarrassing, but she was no longer the young girl he used to know. She'd grown into a very beautiful woman. One who'd apparently had many suitors.

"Do your sisters know?"

His thoughts scrambled for a moment, but she couldn't be asking him whether they knew about his growing feelings for her. "Excuse me?"

"Do your sisters know you have the voice of an angel?"

He scowled at the thought. "They never would have let me get away with not joining in on their little performances if they did."

Celia smiled. "I don't suppose they would have. Well, the secret is out now. They'll insist on singing with you the next time they're here."

"I'm sure I can mangle a song well enough to put them off that idea forever."

Celia laughed. "Were you always this amusing?"

He placed one hand over his heart. "Of course. Are you saying you didn't think I was amusing all those years ago?"

"Always." The warmth in her eyes as she looked up at him had him wondering what else she used to think about him.

"I think my sisters had a little contest between them about who could annoy me more. In fact, I wouldn't be surprised to learn that they still do."

Celia gave a little snort. Her hand flew to her mouth, and he found himself charmed.

"I'm glad you weren't annoyed with me. Honestly, I had the most horrible *tendre* for you." With a slight gasp, she covered her mouth again. "I did not just admit that to you."

He raised a brow, surprised. "How many glasses of wassail have you had tonight?"

She blew out a breath of laughter. "Just the one. I can't even blame my wayward mouth on an excess of spirits."

His gaze settled on her mouth for a moment. He hadn't realized just how plump her lower lip was. He wondered how it would taste if he took it between his teeth.

He shut down those thoughts immediately, but he couldn't stop himself from asking the next question. "So you no longer feel the same way about me. Have I aged so dreadfully over the years?"

She shook her head and swatted at his arm.

"Of course not. But I gave up youthful fantasies some time ago."

"And yet here we are, betrothed."

His reminder had the opposite effect of what he'd hoped to achieve. Celia closed her eyes as though he'd caused her pain.

"I'm so sorry you're being forced to go through this."

"Well, I'm not." He stood and held out a hand to help her from her seat. Then he tucked her hand into his elbow. "I'm sure no one would begrudge you a second glass of wassail. We must enjoy it while we still can."

She beamed up at him. "Yes, please."

MAMA BURST INTO CELIA'S BEDROOM the next morning just as the maid was about to leave.

Her mother's gaze swept over her outfit, a simple yellow day dress with small white flowers. "That will do," she said with a nod before turning to the maid. "My daughter will be going out this morning. Please see that her cloak and gloves are ready. She'll need to stay warm."

The maid curtsied and left the room to do as she'd been bid.

Celia frowned. She hadn't known Lady Thornton had planned any outdoor activities for the day. The estate didn't have a lake, so they wouldn't be going skating.

"Where are we going?"

Mama took hold of her hands, urging her to stand. "Not we. You and Lord Thornton."

Celia frowned. "I'm sure you're mistaken."

Mama let out a long-suffering sigh. "His lordship is going to be visiting his tenants today, something about handing out geese for their Christmas dinners. Apparently he's done it every year since he became aware some have been going without on Christmas."

Celia wasn't surprised to hear that. Thornton had always been generous with his family, so it stood to reason he would extend that kindness to his tenants. Still, her mother's revelation raised the man even further in her estimation.

"Who else will be going?"

"No one else. As his betrothed, he thought it prudent to introduce you to the families that live on his estate."

Given that their betrothal would soon be ending, Celia doubted that was true. "What did you do, Mama?"

"Fine," her mother said, throwing her hands up in the air. "I might have suggested it would be the perfect opportunity. And since some of the other guests were present at the time, he couldn't very well say no."

Celia cringed as she imagined his reaction to her mother's manipulations. "Mama, you should have left it alone."

"Nonsense. Now come, there isn't much time for you to have a quick breakfast before you're to meet him in the front hall."

Celia followed her mother from the room. As they made their way to the breakfast room, she tried to come up with a suitable excuse not to accompany Thornton.

By the time they reached their destination, she'd concluded there was no escaping the task. It would seem selfish in the extreme not to go with her would-be husband as he performed this very worthy errand. Still, she hated that they'd be forced to lie to even more people.

Her cousins were already seated and had saved a space for her. She went to the sideboard and made a quick plate of eggs and toast before joining them.

It was obvious to Celia that they wanted to press her for details about her relationship with Thornton, but her cousins couldn't ignore the people who surrounded them, leaning in a little too close to eavesdrop on their conversation.

Instead they made small talk, mainly sharing their favorite moments from the night before. Chief among them was the moment Thornton had surprised everyone by joining her for "The Twelve Days of Christmas." Conscious of the others listening in, she didn't mind sharing how nervous she'd been before he'd gallantly come to her rescue.

When she finished her eggs, she bid her cousins goodbye and made her way to the front hall. Thornton was already waiting for her.

She didn't miss the way his gaze swept over her and couldn't hold back the blush that crept into her cheeks. "I'm sorry to have kept you waiting," she said when she reached his side.

"I've only just arrived myself, so no need to worry."

The butler had her cloak draped on his arm, and she was surprised when Thornton took it from the man and helped her into it himself before donning his own. Amelia took her gloves from the butler with a smile, then fell into step with Thornton as they left the house.

The sun was out that morning, but a brisk wind had her shivering.

Thornton frowned. "Are you warm enough?"

She nodded. "The wind took me by surprise, but I like the winter air. It's invigorating."

They walked in silence the short distance to where the carriage waited for them. He helped her into the vehicle before climbing in after her. There were packages everywhere, but a small space had been kept clear on each of the bench cushions that faced one another.

Celia settled into her seat and waited for Thornton to do the same before asking, "How many families will we be visiting?"

He smiled at her. She had the impression that he was amused, but she couldn't say why.

"All of them. This is one of my favorite Christmas errands, but I'm sorry you were pressed into joining me."

"It's no trouble at all," she said, doing her best to ignore the way his good humor made him even more attractive. His blue eyes were bright with excitement. "But I do hate that we'll be lying to even more people."

"We won't need to lie. There'll be no reason to announce our betrothal to the tenants."

She realized he was correct. Even if they wondered about her presence, they wouldn't presume to ask. Content with that thought, she settled back into the cushions as the carriage made its way to the first house. To keep from staring at Thornton, she turned to look out the window. He did the same, but she couldn't help but feel the weight of his gaze several times throughout the drive.

HE'D RUN THROUGH THE GAMUT OF EMOTIONS THAT day. First, anticipation for his yearly ritual of visiting his tenants to ensure they would all have a happy Christmas. Then annoyance at Mrs. Rowland's further scheming to ensure he would have to take Celia with him.

When she joined him, however, he found that he enjoyed her company as they shared stories about past Christmases. They fell into an easy rhythm, with him presenting each of his tenants with a large goose for their holiday meal. Celia had insisted on carrying the second box to be delivered, a task the coachman had performed in previous years. It would contain various sweets for the families to enjoy together.

He'd been correct in telling Celia no one would

ask them outright why she was there, but her presence caused more than a few raised eyebrows and knowing glances.

He couldn't deny he was drawn to the way she seamlessly slid into the role his future viscountess would one day perform. And when she'd picked up one toddler who was pulling at her skirts, giving him her attention, the thought occurred to him that she would be a wonderful mother. He was wondering how many children they would have together when his reverie was disturbed by a clap on the shoulder from his tenant. The man nodded toward Celia then said in a low voice, "You've managed to find a good one there."

He let the comment slide, neither confirming nor denying the man's assumption. But the fact of the matter was he'd been thinking the exact same thing.

Celia turned to him and beamed, allowing the toddler to play with one of her curls. When he pulled a little too hard, she wrapped her fingers around his and brought his hand up to her mouth, placing a kiss on his palm. The child's mother swooped in then, apologizing as she took the little boy from her.

Celia laughed. "He wasn't the first, nor will he

be the last child to pull my hair. Please don't concern yourself."

They said their goodbyes then, and he led her from the house.

The emotion that dominated in that moment was confusion because he suddenly realized he enjoyed this task even more with her by his side. He enjoyed *her*. It wasn't just that he was attracted to her, and how could he not be with her blue eyes and blond hair and her luscious figure. He even liked the way the small mole at the corner of her eye highlighted how her eyes crinkled when she smiled. He also liked *her* as a person.

As the morning drew to a close, he found himself staring at her more and more. He didn't realize he was doing it until she reached up and patted her hair when they were seated in the carriage again. "Has a pin fallen out? Heavens, I must look a frightful mess."

"Not at all," he said, embarrassed at being caught acting like an infatuated youth. "I was just thinking that you looked a little cold." It was true that her cheeks and nose were tinged with red and her hair a little windblown, but that had only served to highlight her beauty.

She let out a sigh when the carriage pulled away

from the last house to return to the estate. "I suppose it is time to return to all the speculation and scrutiny."

Because she sat opposite him in the carriage, he could watch her without worrying about being caught. His mouth turned up in amusement. "There was plenty of speculation during our visits today."

"Yes, I know, but no gossip. And for the most part, everyone seemed happy to see me. They weren't looking for scandal."

He hated the flicker of pain that crossed her face. "I didn't realize the whispers bothered you so much."

Her mouth dropped open for a moment. "How could they not? Don't they bother you?"

"My dear, I'm unwed and in possession of a title. The whispers have surrounded me my entire life. They became particularly bad when I turned thirty." He lifted one shoulder in a casual shrug. "You grow accustomed to it."

Her fair curls bounced as she shook her head. "I can't see how. At any rate, the speculation will soon be gone. When the guests leave tomorrow, I'll tell Mama we've decided to end the betrothal."

Her words left a sour taste in his mouth. "Will we?"

"Fine, me." She looked away. "I'll break the engagement. Your reputation will remain intact."

"What of your reputation, Celia?"

She met his gaze. "Mama will be angry, but I'm now of age. Papa set aside some money for me. Of course, he thought it would act as my dowry, but it wasn't specifically set aside for that."

He could only stare at her as he tried to decipher her seemingly casual expression. Was this something she truly wanted, or did she think it was what he wanted? He was beginning to realize it wasn't, but he had to figure out her true feelings.

When he didn't reply, she looked away again. "If things are unbearable at home, I can find a small cottage somewhere where no one knows who I am."

He frowned, hating the idea of her walking away from him and everyone she knew. Sweet young Celia had grown into a temptress, and she wouldn't be safe out in the world alone. Away from him.

"Do we need to end the betrothal right away?"

She stared at him, her lips pressed together, before finally shaking her head. "There will be no point in continuing the pretense once everyone has left."

"What if I told you I think we're being too hasty? That I might want to continue with our betrothal."

Her eyes widened for a moment before narrowing again as she tried to decipher the true meaning behind his words.

"You needn't go to the trouble to protect my reputation."

She was so intent on righting the wrong that her mother had done to the two of them that she couldn't see what was truly happening.

"I'd like to perform a little experiment," he said.

"What type of experiment?" Her lips were still pressed tightly together. He'd have to see whether he could change that.

He indicated the spot next to her on the carriage seat, which was now cleared of packages. She nodded, and he moved into place beside her. They weren't far from the manor house, so they wouldn't have much time before the carriage reached its destination.

He left a respectable distance between them but positioned himself at an angle so he could still watch her as they spoke. He was happy when she mirrored him.

He extended one hand and waited. Celia bit her lower lip, an action that had him wanting to groan, before placing her gloved hand in his. Slowly, giving her time to draw back, he lifted their joined hands and placed a kiss on the patch of bare skin at her wrist. He lingered for a moment, his eyes fixed on hers.

A jolt of anticipation shot through him at the contact, but he held himself back. This was about discovering Celia's true feelings, after all. That anticipation tightened low in his belly when he saw the way her eyes widened at the contact, her breath quickening.

"Am I making you uncomfortable?"

She was silent for a moment, and he feared the worst. He was about to release her hand when she shook her head. "No."

"So you don't mind it when I hold your hand like this? When I kiss your wrist?"

He repeated the movement, and this time her slightly dazed expression was his reward.

"No."

His grip tightened on her hand. "I'd like to kiss you, Celia. May I?"

Her nod was immediate.

He leaned closer, stopping when their faces were only inches apart. "Are you certain you don't mind?"

"Thornton…"

The pleading note in her voice told him clearly that she wanted this as much as he did. He closed the distance between them, pleased when she met him halfway.

He meant to keep the kiss light, not wanting to scare her away. But then she made a soft sound of pleasure, and all his good intentions flew out the window.

The only parts of them that touched were their hands and lips, but he did deepen the kiss. When his tongue touched her bottom lip, she sighed and opened her mouth to accept him.

His skin was on fire, his need for this woman growing with every second that passed as their mouths moved together as if they had done this a thousand times before. She leaned in closer, and her other hand went to his shoulder, but still he resisted the overwhelming need to pull her close.

The sudden jolt of the carriage coming to a halt brought an end to their kiss. He pulled back, as did she. Their gazes locked for several long moments.

He still held one of her hands, and her other hand rested on his shoulder.

"Celia—"

The rattle of the carriage door handle had him releasing her and moving away to preserve Celia's modesty.

Her eyes examined his, and he feared he was about to grab hold of her again, modesty be damned. To prevent that from happening, he stepped down from the carriage first, then turned to help her down.

His fingers tightened on hers to get her attention, but she refused to meet his gaze again. Red tinged her cheeks, but this time he didn't think it was caused by the cool air.

He placed her hand in the crook of his elbow and led her back to the house. When they were a few steps away from the footman who had opened the carriage door, he leaned in close and whispered, "I'd say that experiment was a success."

She didn't reply but the shiver that went through her was all the confirmation he needed that she agreed.

CHAPTER 8

IT WAS TWO DAYS BEFORE CHRISTMAS, which meant his mother's guests would be leaving today. Everyone except Celia and her mother, who had been invited to spend Christmas with them. Celia's cousins would be leaving with one of the other guests, an older couple who had volunteered to see them safely home.

Celia had avoided him for the rest of the day after he'd kissed her, but she wouldn't be able to do so once everyone left.

It seemed that the entire household had woken early and were in the breakfast room that morning. Along with enjoying the grand array of food the servants had set out, many were milling about the room, taking advantage of the last opportunity for conversation before they departed.

His mother sat at one end of the long table and he at the other. And while he had the opportunity to speak to most of the people present, he was acutely aware that Celia was still avoiding him.

She'd arrived late that morning and had given him a quick smile before joining her cousins. He'd caught the way the eldest of the three—Lily?—glanced his way several times during the conversation, which meant she wanted to talk about their relationship. But her frustrated sighs told him Celia was changing the subject.

He didn't regret kissing her yesterday. Her surprise had been genuine, but she'd warmed quickly and had enjoyed it as much as he did.

No, he didn't regret it because it told him exactly what he needed to know. Celia Rowland was drawn to him. She liked him, and he knew that she found him attractive—he was haunted every night by thoughts of how she'd looked at him when he'd left the bed they shared briefly and imaginings of what could have happened if they hadn't been interrupted. He only hoped he'd been successful in convincing her to wait before ending their betrothal.

Gravenhurst was the first to bid his goodbyes to the room at large. Thornton followed him from the room, waiting until they were nearly at the end of the hall before calling out to the man.

Gravenhurst turned and glared at him. "Come to gloat some more?"

The annoyance in the man's voice sparked Thornton's anger. He'd hoped this would be a civil discussion, but it was clear that wasn't to be.

Thornton narrowed his eyes and fixed them on this man who had thought to steal Celia away. "If I hear even one rumor about Miss Rowland, I'll know it came from you."

Gravenhurst scoffed. "What would you be able to do about it?"

Thornton moved closer. "Make no mistake, you will regret it. You might have had friends once, but your biggest allies have turned their backs on you. I can make you a pariah."

Gravenhurst clenched his jaw. Thornton could tell the man wanted to argue but couldn't. His time doing whatever he wanted was in the past. No one would take Gravenhurst's side in a battle between the two of them.

The man gave a stiff nod and turned away. Thornton watched him leave. It took almost a full minute for his anger to cool enough for him to even think about returning to the other guests.

Before he reached the breakfast room, Celia's cousins emerged, followed by the couple who was going to be taking them home. The three curtsied and then hurried past him, giggles trailing in their wake. Thornton bowed to the older couple and turned to watch them go, wondering what it was about him that had amused Celia's cousins.

When he entered the room, most of the guests had stood and were in the process of taking their leave of one another. He moved to stand next to his mother, who stood to one side of the entrance. Together, they thanked the guests for coming and wished them safe travels and a happy Christmas with their families.

Thornton kept glancing at Celia, who now sat beside her mother. He willed her to look up at him, but she kept her gaze averted. That bothered him more than he'd admit because he couldn't tell what she was thinking.

He needed to convince her not to end their betrothal, although he couldn't say why he wanted it so much. She'd grown into a beautiful young woman and had been of age to marry for some time now. The difference in their ages was no longer insurmountable, and he couldn't look at her without wanting to take her into his arms.

She was still sweet, of course, but she also had a determination about her that he admired. And her honor was without question.

Their betrothal had stemmed from an unfortunate turn of events, but he could no longer look at it that way. Because he realized that the misunderstanding that had led to the two of them sharing a bed, albeit briefly, could very well be the best thing that had ever happened to him. That would ever happen to him.

Good grief, he was in love with Celia Rowland.

When the final guest left the room, he strode to Celia's side. When she looked up at him, it seemed as if she was surprised to see him there. He searched her gaze but couldn't tell what she was thinking.

"We'll talk when the guests have all departed," he said.

Celia replied with a nod before looking away again. That simple action told him she still planned to end their betrothal. He wanted to pull her away now, but he had to make an appearance in the foyer to see the guests off.

As if on cue, a footman appeared to his right. "Lady Thornton is waiting for you, my lord."

He gave the man a nod and turned to leave. He didn't miss the satisfaction on Mrs. Rowland's face as he walked past her. It was clear she had no idea what her daughter intended to do. He only hoped he could convince her otherwise.

CELIA WATCHED THORNTON GO WITH A HEAVY heart. There was no sign of the easygoing man she'd seen the day before when they were visiting his tenants. Instead, he'd been so serious.

He confused her. She'd been under the assumption he wanted their forced betrothal to end. Then he'd kissed her, and she'd allowed herself to believe there might just be something more between them. But he hadn't said as much, and just now he hadn't shown any indication that he wanted to court her in earnest.

She took a deep breath to steady her nerves for what was to come. She couldn't allow sentimentality to sway her, and she wouldn't force the man's hand.

After she broke their engagement, she and Mama would leave. She couldn't say when she'd see him again. Now that his sisters were wed and living in the north of England, she would have no excuse to visit again. And she most definitely wouldn't be attending another of his mother's Christmas house parties.

Mama approached to her left and twined her arm through Celia's.

Celia allowed her to lead them from the room so the footmen could clear the remains of the morning meal. But when her mother started to turn toward the foyer, clearly intent on joining Thornton and his mother in bidding the others adieu, Celia tugged on her arm to lead her in the other direction.

Mama tilted her head in question.

"You and I should speak in private before the others return."

Mama considered for a few seconds before nodding her head. "Of course, my dear."

Letting out a breath of relief, Celia led her to the library where they'd be far enough away from the front hall and all the hustle of the departing guests. No one would overhear their conversation.

She had to choose her words carefully. Her mother couldn't guess that she intended to end her pretend engagement to the viscount before the last guest had departed—when it would be too late for her mother to let slip the secret that she and Thornton had been caught together in his bedchamber. Some of the guests were wondering if that had happened, but they didn't know for certain. Celia intended to keep it that way.

But she did need to clear the air with her mother. Her heart was already breaking at the thought of having to end the betrothal. Her mother's scheming to try to force her into a match was a betrayal she had never expected.

She closed the door behind them and turned to face her mother.

"What is the matter, dear?" Her mother's brow was furled in what appeared to be genuine concern. But after learning what Mama had planned with Lord Gravenhurst, Celia wasn't sure she knew this woman at all.

"Lord Thornton told me what happened."

She expected to see guilt, not confusion on her mother's face. "Don't we already know what happened?"

"You can stop pretending, Mama. He told me you'd planned to have Lord Gravenhurst compromise me to force me into marrying him."

Celia saw it then, the flicker of guilt. Then her

mother gave up all pretense and settled into one of the armchairs that were placed before a roaring fire.

"What do you think you know?"

Celia slumped into the chair opposite her mother. A part of her had held on to the hope this had all been a misunderstanding, but now it appeared as though everything was true.

"Were you truly that desperate to have me wed that you—" She had to take a deep breath before she could continue. "You arranged with Lord Gravenhurst to have him compromise me."

Her mother shook her head. "No, it wasn't like that—"

"Lady Thornton overheard you. That was the reason she spirited me away from my room and had me sleep instead in Thornton's room."

"She told you that?"

Celia wanted to laugh at her mother's outrage, but her disappointment was too great. Her mother's betrayal too much. "Of course not. I imagine she wanted to shelter me from the truth that you would go to such lengths to force me into a union I didn't want. She told her son what happened, and he, in turn, told me. To warn me that I needed to be careful in the future."

Her mother leaned forward. "I didn't intend to

allow that to happen. I did have that conversation with him—"

Celia opened her mouth to interrupt, but her mother cut her off.

"No, let me finish. Please."

Celia said nothing and so her mother continued.

"I knew about your feelings for the viscount."

Heat flooded Celia's cheeks. "My youthful infatuation with him, you mean. I outgrew those fantasies years ago."

Her mother's smile was sad. "No, you didn't. You wanted to believe you had, but I could see the truth in your face whenever I brought him up. When I mentioned the invitation to this party, you were excited to attend."

"The party, Mother, not because of the viscount. And what does that have to do with you arranging to have Lord Gravenhurst compromise me?"

Mama winced. "I never should have had that conversation with him. But you should know that I never intended to allow him to go through with it."

Celia rose to her feet and walked away as her disappointment turned to anger. She had to take several deep breaths before turning around to face her mother again.

"I'm going to need you to tell me exactly what you thought would happen. I'd considered myself fortunate to have a parent who didn't feel the need to force me into accepting a marriage proposal I didn't want. But this…" She shook her head. "I am sorely disappointed to discover I was wrong."

Clearly alarmed, Mama leaped to her feet and closed the distance between them. When she reached for her hands, Celia drew back.

Her mother wrapped her arms around her waist. "I made sure to have that conversation with the baron in Lady Thornton's hearing. Then I stood guard down the hall from your room to ensure it didn't happen. I was convinced she was going to confront me about it. I wanted to convince her to work with me to try to make a match between you and her son."

Celia shook her head in disbelief. This sounded more like something her mother would do, but to bring a third party into it? "What were you thinking, Mama? This could have gone horribly wrong. What if Lord Gravenhurst had succeeded?"

"No… no. That never would have happened. If he didn't listen to me and go away, I would have raised the roof before he even got near your room. He would have been forced to leave in disgrace."

"But instead Lady Thornton spirited me away."

"Yes."

"And when Thornton arrived home, you had no difficulty allowing him to enter the same room in which I was sleeping."

Her mother's shoulders slumped. "I was only thinking about how much you cared for him. And I know he was a good brother to Emily and Julia. I thought he would make the perfect husband and that everyone would be happy."

"You played with all our lives, and now Thornton and I have to pay for it."

"But—"

"No, Mama. No matter what happens now, you must promise me you won't interfere."

She could see the moment her mother realized what Celia planned to do. And she could also see her struggle with the desire to ensure the marriage went forward.

"I will never forgive you if you say anything about what happened."

Mama's mouth trembled, then she took a deep breath and nodded.

"You won't interfere anymore? You won't tell

anyone that Thornton has compromised me, no matter what happens?"

"I thought my actions would end in you being happy. Clearly I was wrong. I won't do or say anything."

Celia nodded and walked past her mother. Mama reached for her, but Celia wasn't ready to forgive her. Because of her mother's actions, she'd come to realize that her infatuation with Thornton was, in fact, love. And she would have to set him free.

THE LAST GUEST HAD FINALLY DEPARTED. Thornton stayed in the doorway just long enough to watch the carriage begin to make its way down the drive before leaving to find Celia. He needed to speak to her as soon as possible.

Sensing his mood, his mother didn't try to stop him.

When he looked in the breakfast room, a footman told him she had gone to the library with her mother.

When he entered the library and saw Mrs. Rowland sitting in an armchair, her head in her hands, he feared he was too late. He couldn't make himself ask what had upset her, so he stood there for several moments, fearing the worst.

His mother must have followed him because she entered the library as well. She took one look at Celia's mother and asked if something was the matter.

Mrs. Rowland shook her head, then grimaced. "Celia is angry with me. Given the way I've behaved, I can't say that I blame her."

He wanted nothing more than to chastise the woman himself, but it wasn't his place. And from the devastation on the woman's face, it was clear Celia had already said everything.

"I need to speak with her," Thornton said.

Mrs. Rowland shook her head. "She left me here some time ago. I imagine she's returned to her bedroom."

He began to turn, intent only on finding her, but his mother placed a hand on his arm to stop him. "I can ask one of the maids to go find her."

"There's no need. I'm here."

Thornton turned to see her standing in the doorway. She took a deep breath as she stepped into the room, and Thornton braced himself for what was coming. He tried to meet her gaze, to let her know that they needed to speak before she went forward with this course of action, but she kept her gaze fixed firmly on the floor.

"Celia—"

She shook her head and locked her eyes on her mother, who had risen to stand at her entrance. "His lordship and I have spoken, and we've reached an agreement. We've decided that our betrothal—"

"Should be extended for a period of time."

Celia turned to stare at him, her eyes wide. "But—"

He kept his eyes locked on hers. "If we rush and marry before the start of the new year, tongues will wag in earnest. I would save your daughter from even a hint of gossip."

Celia shook her head, the blond curls that framed her face bouncing with the forceful movement. "That's not what we settled on."

"We should leave them to talk," his mother said. He didn't even turn in her direction as she and Celia's mother left. He could hear their footsteps and murmuring voices disappearing down the hall.

Celia stared at him for several seconds before speaking. "I thought we decided it would be best if I ended the betrothal after everyone left."

"Did we?"

She let out a shaky breath. "Yes, we did. If you're worried about my reputation, no one need know that the engagement is over right away. But we need to set things right with both my mother and yours."

Doubt had him reconsidering their interactions. What if he'd been mistaken about Celia returning his feelings? He wasn't the first man to want to marry her. Perhaps he wouldn't be the last.

"Is the idea of being married to me so abhorrent to you?"

Her eyes widened. "No, of course not. It would be an honor to be your wife."

He took a step closer. "Just an honor? Nothing else?"

She looked away.

"Celia?"

She let out a sigh and met his gaze again. "I've come to… care for you. You're a good man, and you don't deserve to be forced into a marriage you don't want."

He could feel the doubts scattering with every word she spoke. "What about what you want? Do you want this marriage?"

She looked down at her hands, which she clutched at her waist. "It doesn't matter what I want. We're in this position because of my mother's scheming. You shouldn't have to suffer for it."

He could only shake his head in disbelief. "And what if I don't want you to end things?"

She sighed again. "I must be the one to end things so you can move forward without anyone questioning your honor."

He took another step closer. She still couldn't see what he was saying. "I think we should get married." He placed a hand over hers, causing her to stop fidgeting. "I *want* to marry you, Celia. Unless, of course, there is someone else…"

Her brows drew together, and she stared at him. He began to worry that sweet Celia's heart was already engaged elsewhere.

"No," she said when she finally spoke. "There is no one else."

"And you don't find the idea of marrying me objectionable?"

She shook her head, a look of wonder creeping onto her face. "Only a fool would object to marrying you."

"Well, then Celia Rowland, since you are no fool, I am asking you to please do me the honor of becoming my wife."

Her mouth gaped open, then snapped closed. "But my mother… you must hate her."

He shrugged. "I'm not overly fond of her, no.

And I question her lack of judgment in the way she was going about trying to find you a husband. But my feelings for her are irrelevant. It is you I wish to marry, not your mother."

She examined him, her gaze locked on his, and he knew she was looking for any sign he might be lying to her. She wouldn't find any.

"Are you sure?"

He smiled. "It appears we're going to get our fondest wishes for Christmas this year."

Her head tilted to one side. "I find it difficult to believe you wished for a wife."

He shrugged. "It was always going to happen, but not quite so soon. Then I happened upon a certain bundle in my bed and found myself wanting to see her there again and every night after that."

Celia laughed, and the sound sparked joy within him because it meant she was going to accept him.

"You could have any woman in England."

"That might be a slight exaggeration, but it doesn't matter. I want you. And if I must, I'll compromise you again."

When he opened his arms, she moved into them and raised her head for a kiss. "By all means, my lord."

He took her mouth on a laugh, but all amusement fled when she sighed and pressed her body against his.

Finally, he had Celia Rowland exactly where he wanted her. The last thing he wanted was to let her go, but the sound of voices increasing in volume told him their mothers were returning.

He let her go with great reluctance but tucked her hand into his arm. They were both smiling when their mothers returned.

"Perhaps a spring wedding?" He glanced down at Celia.

"Spring sounds wonderful," she said, beaming up at him.

CHAPTER 10

S PRING DID SOUND WONDERFUL, but it also sounded so far away. She and her mother would be spending Christmas with the Thorntons before returning to their homes. From that point forward, she would only see the viscount when he called on her.

After the bustle of the past few days, it was nice to spend a quiet day together. It was also frustrating because Mama and Lady Thornton seemed to go out of their way to ensure she and Thornton weren't alone together.

She was still angry at her mother, but she would forgive her in time. Everything had worked out beyond her wildest expectations, after all.

After dinner, they made their way to the

drawing room. Mama and Mrs. Rowland sat off to one side, snippets of their conversation catching Celia's ear. They were discussing the need to read the banns and when they should have the wedding.

Thornton, who sat next to her on the settee, could only shake his head. "They seem to be more excited than us."

She shook her head. "That isn't possible."

He smiled at her, and she had to fight the urge to swoon.

"I almost didn't come to Mother's house party this year and put it off as long as possible. I wasn't in the mood for all the singing and festivities. And after our first meeting—well, I wasn't in the best of moods that night."

She winced. "At least now we are free from the prying eyes of people who wanted to dissect our relationship."

"Indeed," Thornton said. "I must say that my sisters will be sad not to have been here."

"Was there a reason they didn't come? I was looking forward to seeing them."

"Apparently they were snowed in. I hope they're able to arrive for the new year. Mother will be sad if she doesn't see them at all for the season."

Celia looked over to where Lady Thornton was

laughing with her mother. "She doesn't look sad to me."

He laughed. "No, I don't suppose that she does. But that will change soon enough when you and your mother have gone home." He turned back to her, his gaze softening. "As will I. I'd originally planned to return to London after the new year, although I'm not sure why. Most of my friends have returned to their own homes, and the city holds little in the way of entertainments of late. Surrey seems to hold much more interest for me this year."

From the amusement that lit Thornton's eyes, it was possible she might have swooned just a little. Others had paid her similar compliments, but only this man could get such a reaction from her.

A hint of melancholy touched her heart at the reminder their time together, for the near future, would soon come to an end. "If you change your mind after I leave, you must tell me. We can still end the betrothal. And come spring and the beginning of the season, I'm sure there will be much more interesting gossip to entertain people."

He frowned, but his voice was light when he said, "Am I going to have to compromise you in actual fact to keep you from trying to escape?"

She must have drunk too much wassail that

evening. Why else would she have leaned closer to him and said, her voice matching his low pitch, "Perhaps you should."

When she realized what she had just proposed, heat crept into her face. But instead of being scandalized, Thornton's gaze locked on to hers and seemed to heat. "Perhaps I should."

She needed to get away from this man before she said or did something that would embarrass her further. It was taking every ounce of her willpower not to close the small gap between them and kiss him. If their mothers weren't in the room, she might have done just that.

A quick glance in their parents' direction assured her they hadn't overheard their conversation. With a soft sigh, she stood. Thornton followed suit, and all eyes turned to her.

"I think I'll be retiring for the night."

"Are you all right, my dear?" Lady Thornton asked.

She rushed to reassure her. "I believe the late nights from the past few days have finally caught up with me."

She turned to curtsy to Thornton. It was almost impossible to believe this man would soon be her husband.

He took hold of one hand and placed a kiss on her wrist, his warm lips resting momentarily on the exposed skin above her glove, his gaze locking on to hers. "Good night, Celia."

Flustered, she dipped into a curtsy and all but fled from the room, chastising herself all the way back to her bedroom. As her conversation played over in her mind, she couldn't hold back a groan of embarrassment.

She'd invited him to compromise her. What had happened to her common sense? Even worse, what if Thornton thought her a wanton?

She tossed and turned for some time, unable to dispel her worries, before finally falling asleep.

SHE HAD TO BE DREAMING. WHY ELSE WOULD Thornton be in her bedroom, sitting on the edge of her bed?

She rose to a sitting position and stared at him for several long seconds before finally finding her voice. "This is a dream."

Thornton leaned closer and placed a hand on her cheek. His thumb stroked along her lower lip. "Not a dream," he said softly.

The shiver that went through her body gave credence to his words.

She stared up at him. "You came. I never imagined you would."

"After that invitation, I'd be a fool to stay away. But I won't proceed unless you tell me you want this as much as I do. We can wait until we're wed to go any further."

She had no idea what instinct led her to take his thumb into her mouth, but the way his gaze darkened as she sucked on his thumb told her that he didn't mind. He slid his hand away after several seconds.

"I am a hairbreadth away from losing control. You must give me the words—I don't want to presume."

"Please stay." Two days ago she never would have imagined uttering those words, but in that time she'd come to realize just how much she cared for this man. She wanted to give him everything.

He drew in a shuddering breath. "You know what I am proposing?"

She nodded. "That we make love. And yes, I would very much like you to continue."

The press of his mouth on hers was her answer, and a thrill of expectation shot through her.

But then he kissed her the way he had in the carriage, sliding his tongue into her mouth to deepen the kiss. She'd always been slightly uncomfortable with the idea that men kissed in this way when Thornton's sisters had teased her about how delightful it was after they wed. She hadn't believed them, but she'd been very wrong to doubt them.

The way Thornton's tongue slid against hers was more sinful than she could have imagined, and she moaned in a way that should have shocked her.

He pulled back and gazed down at her, his eyes dark, reflecting the need she could feel growing within her.

"If you don't want me to——"

She dragged his mouth down to hers before he could continue, afraid he would disappear just as quickly as he'd appeared. "Don't you dare stop," she said against his lips before sliding her own tongue along his lower lip.

With a groan, he reciprocated, and they spent several long, delicious minutes kissing.

She let out a small shriek when he shifted her onto her back, but he swallowed the sound before pulling back to gaze down from where he hovered over her.

"This is your last chance to ask me to stop."

She shook her head. "Ravish me, my lord."

One corner of his mouth curved upward in a wicked smile. "You have no idea how much I've wanted this," he said, dropping a kiss on her cheek before moving to kiss the side of her throat.

Oh, she had an idea because she'd wanted it as much as he did. Wanted him. But she'd never even allowed herself to dream it was possible. Now she could recognize that the reason she'd never been able to settle on one of the many men her mother had paraded before her was because none of them could compare to the fantasy of this man.

But he wasn't a dream. This was very real.

She arched under his touch when he cupped one of her breasts.

"You've definitely grown up, Celia." He dropped kisses along the bodice of her nightgown and then gave the material a sharp tug. She'd hated how large her breasts had become. Hated how men seemed fixated on that part of her. But now, as they were bared to Thornton's hot gaze, she found herself disliking them a little less.

And when he took one of her nipples into his mouth, white-hot pleasure streaked through her. Words failed her as he took his time lavishing kisses over her breasts. She made a soft sound of disappointment when he rose to stand and struggled up onto her elbows.

"Don't leave."

"I have no intention of leaving. But first…" He strode over to the door and turned the lock.

Shock took over as she realized that anyone could have walked in on them. She tried not to picture her mother flinging open the door as Thornton was kissing her breasts, unable to hold back a twinge of embarrassment at her wanton behavior. Thank heavens at least one of them was still thinking.

He jammed the chair from her dressing table under the doorknob for good measure, and she stifled a giggle. Apparently the viscount was picturing the same scenario as her.

When he turned to face her, his brows were drawn into a frown. She realized she'd drawn the bed sheet up to cover herself and released her grip on the fabric, allowing it to slide down to her waist.

"Much better," he said.

The heat in his gaze did much to ease her embarrassment. What made it disappear altogether was watching him begin to disrobe.

With each garment, her anticipation grew. She'd already seen his bare chest that first evening.

This time, she didn't look away as he watched her reaction when he finally drew his shirt over his head.

More than anything, she couldn't wait to touch him. No, this wasn't a dream because her imagination wasn't this good.

Her breath hitched when his hands moved to the fall of his trousers. He stopped, one brow raised in question. He was asking her if he should stop. In answer, she took a deep breath, stood, and allowed her nightgown to fall in a puddle around her feet.

His movements quickened then, as though he couldn't wait to finally shed the last of his clothing.

When he stood completely naked before her, she couldn't stop the heat from rising to her cheeks. He was hard, his erection rising away from him. She'd heard about this too but found herself hesitating, unsure what to do now.

She wanted to touch him all over but didn't know if she should. She couldn't help but think that perhaps she should get back onto the bed and pretend she wasn't experiencing the sinful emotions that seemed to have taken hold of her.

She didn't realize she'd closed her eyes—she could still see him clearly in her mind's eye—until she felt his finger under her chin, tilting her face up to meet his.

She opened her eyes and his gazed bored into hers. "What are you thinking?"

She wanted to demur, to tell him it was nothing. But if she was going to marry this man, she didn't want to begin their relationship on a foundation of lies.

"I'm wrestling with what I want to do and what I think I should be doing."

"Meaning…?"

"I'm feeling decidedly unladylike. I want to touch you, but I'm not sure if I should."

By way of reply, he took hold of her hand and placed it squarely in the center of his chest. The heat rising from his skin almost scorched her hand.

"I plan to touch you *everywhere*, and I hope you'll reciprocate."

Almost of their own volition, her eyes dropped to his member before rising again to meet his.

He answered the question she couldn't ask. "Yes."

Never in a million years would she have thought herself brave enough for this. But she wasn't with just any man. She was with Thornton, and in his presence, she felt as though she could do no wrong.

Aside from that, he clearly wanted her to touch him, but he would never force her.

She started slowly, spreading her hands across the hard muscles of his chest, then across his abdomen. She hesitated, and he must have thought she would go no further for he took her mouth in another searing kiss and tugged her closer so their bodies aligned. She gasped at the feel of his skin burning into hers. Kissing this man was pleasurable when fully clothed, but when they were both bare, the pleasure was indescribable.

He cupped one of her breasts again, and in an act of bravery, she reached down to grasp his manhood. His hiss of breath had her releasing him again immediately.

"I apologize—"

By way of reply, he grasped her hand again and brought it back down to encircle him.

"I was surprised, Celia, not in pain. It is more painful if you *don't* touch me."

CHAPTER 11

SHE WAS GOING TO BE THE DEATH OF HIM. He hadn't expected it, so when she wrapped her small hand around his length, the intense pleasure took him by surprise. But he most definitely did not want her to stop.

"Don't scream," he said before scooping her into his arms and carrying her to the bed. The feel of her smooth skin against his left him heady with need.

He placed her on the bed's surface with great care before lying down next to her. Then he proceeded to touch every inch of that skin he could reach, allowing his mouth to explore her glorious breasts. She reciprocated in kind, leaving behind her reservations.

When he couldn't wait any longer, he rose onto his arms over her. He should have prepared her with his hands or with his mouth but he feared he wouldn't have the restraint to do so without spilling all over the sheets. And he most definitely wanted to be inside her tonight.

He stared down at her, enjoying the way her breath came out in short pants as she toyed with the hair at the nape of his neck.

"This next part is going to hurt. I'm sorry."

She smiled up at him, no hint of trepidation in her eyes.

"I know. But I also have it on good authority that it will be even more pleasurable afterward."

He didn't want to know who'd shared such information with her. If it was one of his sisters… His mind shied away from completing that thought, and he refocused on Celia.

The first touch of his member against her wet folds had both of them releasing soft sounds of pleasure. Thankfully, she was wet. Her face scrunched in pain when he sank into her, and it took all his strength not to move.

She was tight, and he had to master himself so he wouldn't spill immediately. He had no idea what it was about this woman, but she affected him like no one else.

A full minute must have passed before she tilted her head to one side. "Is that all there is?"

His bark of laughter surprised them both. "No, my sweet Celia, there is more. I wanted to make sure you were no longer in pain."

She raised one of her legs, settling it over his, and he let out a groan as he sank deeper into her.

"I think I'm ready. It doesn't hurt anymore."

Thank heavens for that. He placed a hand below the knee of her leg and hitched it higher to encircle his hips. She followed suit with her other leg, cradling him within her body.

He couldn't resist kissing her again as he began to move. She was still at first, but within moments was moving with him. A soft mewl escaped her lips, and he leaned back to look at her, worried she was still in pain. But the expression on her face was that of a woman who very much enjoyed what they were doing.

Knowing how sensitive her breasts were, he began to knead one as he continued to thrust, doing everything in his power to move with care. She might not be in pain, but she would be sensitive.

"Isaac," she said on a low moan.

The sound of his name on her lips sent a jolt of pleasure straight to his heart. Very few people used his Christian name, not even his mother. But he found that he very much liked it.

He wouldn't be able to last much longer. Keeping his weight on one arm, he released her breast with reluctance and moved his hand between them. He circled that sensitive area above where they were joined, doing everything in his power to ensure she found her release before he did.

After only a few strokes he was rewarded by her swift intake of breath, and then her entire body clenched. The feel of her wrapping even tighter around his length caused him to lose what little control he had left, and he spilled inside her body.

They stayed like that for several long moments. When her eyes opened, her gaze was wide with wonder.

"I never expected…" She gave her head a shake, letting out a small laugh. "I suppose you'll have to marry me now."

He rolled to one side, taking her with him and tucking him into his side. "It would be my pleasure and greatest honor."

Thankfully, that would be soon. He'd been so

caught up in her pleasure and in his own that he hadn't pulled out of her as he'd planned.

Perhaps he'd be a father within the year. The thought should have filled him with horror, but instead a smile spread over his face as he pictured Celia round with his child. But he couldn't risk that happening before they were wed.

"We'll arrange to have the banns read right away and be married in a month."

She lifted her head, her radiant smile doing much to ease the guilt he felt at not being able to wait. "Spring was too far away," she said. "I was never going to last that long without you."

He twined his hand in her hair and returned her smile. "I couldn't agree more."

HE STAYED IN CELIA'S BED MUCH LONGER THAN HE'D intended, and only managed to make it back to his room just before the sun began to rise.

No sooner had he crept into his own bed than his valet entered. The man's eyes swept over the bed, which wasn't nearly as rumpled as normal. He raised a brow but didn't say a word as he headed for the dressing room.

"We have guests, and your presence has been requested in the drawing room."

Thornton frowned, wondering which one of his mother's guests had returned. It had better not be Gravenhurst.

"Who is it?" He rose and joined his valet in the adjoining room, watching as the man picked out each item of clothing for the day.

"The footman didn't say. Apparently it's supposed to be a surprise."

Thornton grinned. That must mean that at least one of his sisters had made it down, which would please their mother to no end. That's all she wanted for Christmas, after all—to see her family all together for at least a few days.

When he was finished dressing, he thanked his valet and headed for the drawing room. The sound of voices echoing down the hallway told him that his guess had been correct. Even better, when he entered the room he saw that both Emily and Julia were there, as were their husbands.

"Isaac!" Both his sisters leaped from their seats and barreled into him, embracing him from each side.

Emily gave him a mock frown when she pulled back. "We'd hoped to surprise you, but it seems you've taken the wind out of our sails. I can't believe you and Celia are to be married!"

He looked over to where Celia was sitting on the settee, a serene smile on her face.

"Within the month. We've decided to have the banns read and then have the ceremony the following week."

Julia looked over at her husband. "We hadn't planned to stay that long, but perhaps we can change our plans."

Mother was beaming from her seat next to Celia on the settee. "We do still have some of your gowns here for your visits. I'm sure we can manage."

Emily placed one hand over her belly. "I imagine they'll still fit, but perhaps they'll need to be let out by the end of the month."

"Congratulations, Emily," Thornton said, dropping a kiss on his sister's cheek before turning to congratulate his brother-in-law.

Mother and Celia rushed to Emily's side while he greeted the two men.

"I think you've managed to overshadow our announcement," Thornton said, clapping Emily's husband on the shoulder.

"Nonsense. I'm surprised you didn't hear the

shrieks when your sisters learned about your betrothal. It was almost deafening."

Thornton turned to watch the women, who were huddled together, chattering away.

He didn't realize he was staring until Julia sidled up next to him and elbowed him. "I recognize that look. You're in love."

Celia joined them and smiled at him.

Emily sighed loudly. "We're so happy for the two of you. Celia has fancied you for as long as I can remember."

Color rose in her face, and Thornton smiled fondly at her.

"Well, back then she was far too young for me to think of in that way. But trust me, I took notice of her right away upon our meeting again."

"You must share all the details," Emily said. His sisters each took one of his arms. "But first, breakfast. I'm starving."

Celia lifted one shoulder in a small shrug, and he couldn't help but wonder if she would, indeed, tell his sisters everything. He tried not to think about what else she would share with them as he led his sisters and the small group to the breakfast room.

CHAPTER 12

Christmas morning

CELIA WOKE WITH A SMILE ON HER FACE.

Everyone had stayed up into the early hours of the morning to welcome in Christmas. The pianoforte had been brought into the drawing room, and they'd sung carols for a good portion of the evening, played whist, and chatted. Finally, Emily had announced she was exhausted. Declaring that she didn't want to see anyone until midmorning at the earliest, she'd retired with her husband. After her departure, everyone had wandered off to their own bedrooms.

Celia hadn't expected Thornton to join her—he

wouldn't risk it a second time. Still, unable to fall asleep, she'd waited up for some time.

It was silly, but she missed him. Now that they had a future together, she couldn't wait for it to start.

She called for a maid, who helped her to dress and pin up her hair. She was on her way downstairs to join the others for breakfast when it occurred to her that this would be her future home.

She stood in the doorway for several moments, taking in the scene before her. Thornton and his family were seated around the breakfast table, talking and laughing. He was teasing Emily by proposing the most ridiculous of names for her baby, and with each suggestion, both she and Julia laughed even louder. Her two friends had always meant the world to her, and joy unfurled in her chest at the knowledge they would soon be her sisters.

Lady Thornton saw her first and called out a welcome.

Every eye in the room turned to her, everyone calling out their own greetings. She'd been the subject of similar scrutiny when Lady Thornton's guests were still in residence, but she felt no unease with these people who were soon to be her family.

Her gaze settled on Thornton, and she didn't care that her smile could only be called sappy.

She caught the way Emily and Julia were grinning at her as well as the dowager viscountess. When Thornton rose and approached her, she realized they were waiting to see her reaction.

Thornton stopped before her, and she gazed up at him, curious. "What is happening?"

He pointed up, and it was then she saw the mistletoe hanging in the doorway. Thornton plucked a white berry from the small branch before leaning down to place a quick peck to the side of her lips. When he pulled back, his gaze was intense. "Walk with me for a moment."

Making a point not to look at anyone else in the room, she nodded and took his arm. He led them to the drawing room.

He moved to stand in front of her, staring down at her. She couldn't help but take note of just how handsome he was, as she did every time she saw him. She didn't think it was possible for him to appear otherwise.

"That mistletoe wasn't there before," she said, thinking about the knowing looks from Thornton's sisters and feeling a twinge of embarrassment.

"No. Mother's never been one to put a woman in a position to attract attention she doesn't want."

She shivered, imagining Lord Gravenhurst taking advantage of such an opportunity. "But she's changed her mind now that the guests have gone?"

One corner of his mouth lifted in a knowing smirk. "I might have arranged that myself."

She could only shake her head in disbelief. "I should admonish you for embarrassing me like that, but in truth I didn't mind." She hesitated a moment before adding, "I missed you last night."

His blue eyes darkened. "And I you. But we've already taken one chance. I don't want you to fall with child before the wedding."

She sighed with disappointment but knew he was right.

He took one of her hands in his. "I didn't have anything to give you for Christmas."

He placed his other hand against her cheek, and she nuzzled into his palm.

"Nor I you. I expected to spend Christmas day at home."

He shook his head. "You've already given me so much. Given how our betrothal started, and your belief that I wished to be rid of you—"

"I—" She started to interrupt, but he moved his

hand and placed his fingers against her lips. He didn't drop them until she nodded to indicate she would allow him to finish.

He reached into his coat pocket to retrieve something. "I *didn't* have anything to give you when I arrived. I never imagined I'd find my future bundled underneath my bedsheets that first night. So I spoke to my mother, and together we decided there was only one thing to do."

She tilted her head in curiosity but had no idea to what he was referring.

He held out his hand. Nestled in his palm was a delicate gold ring with a rather large pearl mounted on it.

She gasped. It wasn't customary for a man to give his intended a betrothal ring, but she had to admit that his gesture touched the romantic inside her.

"This ring belonged to my grandmother. My father gave it to my mother when they became engaged, and now I'm passing it on to you with my mother's blessing."

She opened her mouth, then closed it again, too overcome with emotion to speak.

He smiled and raised her left hand. "We might need to have it resized." With care, he slid the ring onto her finger, and to both their surprise, it fit as though it were made for her.

She stared down at it for several moments, overcome with love for this man. When she met his gaze again, she could see a slight frown where before he'd been happy.

"Of course, I can buy something more ornate. I know it is a simple setting—"

This time, it was she who placed her fingers over his lips to stop him from continuing. "I will not have you saying anything negative about my ring. It is perfect… and so are you. I love you, Isaac."

His concern disappeared, replaced by a doting expression she didn't think she'd ever tire of seeing.

"I love you too, Celia. Happy Christmas."

He kissed her then, and she returned it without hesitation. She didn't care who walked in on them. She loved this man, and she wanted the whole of England to know.

EPILOGUE

November 1817

CELIA MADE HER WAY to the drawing room, pleased with the excuse to escape Lady Thornton's attentions, even if only for a little while. Her mother-in-law's annual Christmas party was only one month away, and she'd wanted Celia to feel as though her input was valued on every detail of the upcoming house party.

Every minute detail.

Honestly, it was an annual affair. How many decisions needed to be made? She'd wanted to tell the dowager viscountess to do what she'd done every year, but the look of excitement on the woman's face had stopped her.

But now her cousin Lily was here for a visit and Celia had leaped at the excuse to take a moment away from the small stack of menus the house-keeper had asked her to approve.

Celia smiled as she swept into the room. Lily seemed to be deep in thought and so she dropped onto the settee next to her cousin. "I'm so glad you're here. If I had to look at another menu, I was going to scream."

Lily let out a sigh and unease settled over Celia. "Has something happened?"

Lily bit her lip. "I needed to speak with you."

Celia grasped her cousin's hand. "Of course. You can tell me anything."

"It's about Lord Seaford. I think he's going to propose."

Celia frowned, wondering at Lily's obvious concern. "Would that be so bad? He's been courting you for several months now. I thought you liked him."

Lily leaned back against the settee and closed her eyes. "I thought so, as well."

"Then what is the issue?"

Lily met her gaze. "You are."

Celia shook her head, confused by her cousin's

words. "Me? I've said nothing about Lord Seaford. I barely know the man. He seemed nice enough when Isaac introduced us this past spring. Very respectable."

"That is the problem. I don't want someone respectable."

Her cousin wasn't making any sense. "You're going to have to explain this to me. Surely, you're not saying you want to wed someone disreputable?"

Lily blew out a long breath. "No, of course not. But I want a man who looks at me the way your husband looks at you. A man who loves me."

A twinge of dismay went through her at Lily's obvious distress. "That can come in time. It took Isaac and me a little while to realize our feelings for one another."

Lily laughed. "You've had a *tendre* for Thornton for as long as I can remember."

Heat rose in her cheeks. "I won't deny that's true. But I also know that you feel the same way about Lord Seaford. Or at least I thought you did."

"He's so polite, almost distant with me. So staid and careful. I want someone who will sweep me off my feet."

"Well, I can tell you that scandal is highly overrated. I was very dismayed when Thornton was first forced into declaring we were going to be wed."

"But it worked out in the end."

"Yes, but what if it hadn't? I believe Lord Seaford is going about this the right way, giving the two of you the chance to know one another."

Lily leaned forward. "I can't deny that he's very handsome."

Celia lowered her voice. "Don't repeat this to my husband, but I think so as well. And…" She hesitated, unsure if she should continue.

"And what?"

"Isaac was dismayed when he heard that the Earl of Seaford was courting you. Apparently, he has a reputation for being a rake."

Lily sank back into the settee's cushions again. "That makes it even worse. Perhaps he's worked through whatever youthful wildness he possessed and now that he's ready to settle down, he's become boring. He has always been circumspect with me."

"Has he kissed you?"

Lily let out a snort. "He's kissed my hand. Does that count?"

Oh dear. Perhaps her husband had been mistaken about Seaford's reputation. "I can't tell you what to do. Have you shown him you want him to kiss you?"

Lily shook her head, her blonde curls bouncing in joyous counterpoint to her somber mood. "How would I do that? I've smiled, laughed, leaned in a little close to him. Nothing."

Now it was Celia's turn to sigh. "How long has he been courting you?"

"Six months!"

Celia winced. "What is your heart telling you?"

The corners of Lily's mouth turned down. "I like him a great deal. And until I'd seen the way Thornton behaves around you, I thought we could make a good match. But I've discovered that I'm selfish. I want him to look at me the way your husband looks at you and I fear that will never happen."

Celia pulled her cousin into a quick hug. "The only advice I can give you is to listen to your heart."

"What if my heart and my head can't agree?"

Celia wished she could ease her cousin's dismay. "I'm afraid that only you can answer that question."

I hope you enjoyed reading Celia and Thornton's story. Lily and the Earl of Seaford's story is next! You can pre-order *A Highwayman for Christmas* now.

To find out what I am working on and when I have a new release available, sign up for my newsletter here.

SNEAK PEEK OF LOVING THE
MARQUESS

Turn the page for a sneak peek of Suzanna Medeiros's book, *Loving the Marquess*. It is book one in her bestselling LANDING A LORD series…

EXCERPT—LOVING THE MARQUESS

He wasn't supposed to fall in love with her...

The Marquess of Overlea's plan was perfect. Marry the desperate Louisa Evans, saving her and her siblings from ruin, and produce an heir. But when he proposes, Nicholas doesn't tell her the real reason they must wed so quickly.

They are married when Louisa learns the Marquess doesn't intend to father his future heir himself. Drawn to her new husband in a way she never expected, Louisa has no intention of agreeing to his scandalous proposition. Instead, she shows him that what is developing between them goes far beyond a typical marriage of convenience.

Nicholas never imagined he would fall in love with Louisa. Despite the distance he tries to put between them, one thing soon becomes clear—he will never allow another man to touch her. Even if it dooms his family's future.

CHAPTER 1

Kent
1806

A KNOCK AT THE DOOR in the middle of the night never brought good news. Casting a longing glance at the welcoming bed she'd been about to sink into, Louisa Evans tied the sash of her dressing gown. Pushing aside the weariness that dragged at her, she hurried downstairs.

She expected to find one of her neighbors when she opened the door and was surprised to find, instead, a stranger. A very tall man with dark hair who sagged against the door frame, his eyes closed. She shivered as the cool autumn air cut through her nightgown and dressing gown.

"Can I help you?" she asked.

When he didn't reply, she wondered if he were foxed and had somehow stumbled across their cottage. She placed a hand on his arm to gain his attention and repeated her question.

His eyes opened and he pinned her with a gaze that was dark and penetrating.

"I require assistance…" he managed to say before closing his eyes again.

He swayed slightly and started to slide down the doorframe. Moving instinctively, Louisa had her shoulder under his arm in a moment, steadying him as he collapsed. He was much larger than she, and for a second she thought she would collapse with him.

She straightened and stared down, stunned, at where he sat propped against the doorframe. Hesitating only a moment, she leaned over him to smell his breath and detected a faint hint of alcohol. She brought a hand to his forehead and was alarmed to find he had a fever.

Another blast of the night air, uncharacteristically cold this early in September, had her shivering in earnest now. She would have to move the stranger inside and close the door. She didn't know what was wrong with him, but with his fever he couldn't afford to catch a chill. She wasn't strong enough, however, to carry him inside on her own.

Her decision made, she hurried upstairs and rapped on her brother's door. When he didn't answer, she entered the room and shook him awake.

"What's the matter?" he mumbled, his eyes still closed.

"I need your help. There's a man downstairs who is ill. He collapsed on our doorstep."

John jolted awake at the mention of the stranger. At eighteen, he was seven years younger than her, but since their father had died, he'd decided it was his duty to protect the family.

He dressed quickly and followed her downstairs to where the man sat, still propped up, in their doorway.

"Who is he?"

Louisa shook her head. "I don't know, but he's ill and the cold can't be good for him. Help me bring him inside so I can close the door."

They managed to rouse the man enough to help him to his feet, supporting his weight between them. He was unsteady and their progress was slow, but at her insistence they managed to bring him to her room, still warm from her recently banked fire. He collapsed on her bed with a groan.

"I'll see to his comfort," she told John. "I saw a horse outside that must belong to our guest. The animal will need to be cared for."

John set his shoulders and she knew he was going to insist that she look after the horse. She cut him off before he could protest the impropriety of the situation.

"Do you actually believe this man is in any condition to do me harm?"

Her brother hesitated, but it was clear the stranger had lost consciousness. Grumbling something under his breath about bossy sisters, he turned and left to see to the horse.

Louisa occupied herself with rebuilding a fire in the small fireplace before turning to look at the man lying on her bed. Despite her assurances to her brother, she was nervous. She'd nursed their father during his long illness, but caring for this man was nowhere near the same.

She approached the bed and looked down at him, and her heart fluttered as she realized just how handsome he was. His hair was a dark brown, almost black, framing a face that had no doubt caused many other hearts to beat faster, as well. Despite his fever, he was very pale, his skin drawn taut over high cheekbones and a strong jaw that was already showing a hint of stubble.

She swallowed hard as her gaze traveled down the length of him. He was asleep, but his presence filled the room. She shook her head to clear it and turned away, telling herself that caring for this man would be no different than caring for her father as she went to her washstand and poured water from the pitcher into the washbasin. Concentrating on the familiar task, she set the basin on her bedside table, dipped a washcloth into the water, and wrung it out. Her hands were not quite steady as she washed his face, hoping the cool water would bring him a measure of comfort. Her movements were brisk, but slowed when he moaned. His eyes opened and she froze as his black, inscrutable gaze caught and held hers.

She was spiraling downward, drowning in twin pools of darkness. The heat in the room seemed to increase as a flush spread through her body. The seconds ticked by, seeming to stretch into minutes.

Without another sound, the stranger's eyes closed again. She dragged in a shaky breath and shook off the paralysis that had stolen over her. She could not, however, shake off her sense of unease.

Her hands were still shaking when she dropped

the damp cloth into the basin. Pushing aside her trepidation, she moved to the bottom of the bed to remove his boots. She hesitated only a moment before placing one hand on the heel of the black leather molded to his right leg and the other on his knee. A jolt of awareness surged through her at the contact and she jerked back. Her gaze flew to the stranger's face, and she breathed a sigh of relief when she saw he was still asleep. She would have died of mortification if he'd seen her foolish reaction to touching him.

She tugged off his boots before turning her attention to removing his coat, but she knew her bravery did not extend that far. Her bedcovers were already turned down and it took only a couple of tugs to free them completely from under his legs. Concentrating on the blankets and not on his form, she covered him before exhaling the breath she'd been holding. Most of him was now hidden from sight, but she found it impossible to ignore the keen sense of awareness brought on by the knowledge that a very attractive man now slept in her bed.

Trying to ignore the less than chaste thoughts that rose, unbidden, to her mind, Louisa retrieved a blanket for herself from the trunk at the foot of her bed and settled into a chair to wait. When John returned from seeing to their unexpected guest's horse, he tried to insist on taking her place, but if the stranger's condition took a turn for the worse, John wouldn't know what to do. He helped her to remove the man's coat and loosen his cravat before returning to his own room, but only after extracting her promise to fetch him when the man woke.

It was a long night. The stranger's slumber was restless—interrupted, at first, by frequent bouts of thrashing and murmured words that were indecipherable. Eventually, he settled into a deep sleep and she was able to close her eyes and get some rest. She had just drifted off when a low moan woke her. She struggled up from her cramped position in the armchair by the bedside, and her blanket slid to the floor.

"Papa? Do you need anything?" she asked, disoriented after being pulled from the middle of a strange dream.

But the man lying in the bed, her bed, wasn't her father. She was confused for a moment and then the memories rushed back. After a year of failing health, her father had finally succumbed to death six months before. She leaned back in the chair and examined the stranger more closely in the faint morning light. She hadn't dreamt him after all.

The fire had long since gone out and she shivered in the cool morning air. She picked up the blanket from where it had fallen, wrapped it around her shoulders, and took the few steps to the bed. Leaning forward, she laid a hand on the man's forehead and breathed a sigh of relief when she found his temperature was normal.

She looked over at the window where the first rays of morning light were already creeping over the horizon and sighed softly. So much for a good night's rest, she thought as she began to work the kinks from her knotted muscles.

Nicholas Manning's head was killing him, but he was used to that. He raised a hand to rub at his temples, hoping to massage away the pain. Unable to stop himself, his thoughts went back to that time a few years ago, before his parents' deaths. They'd been content, their love still evident even after more than thirty years of marriage. But then his father started complaining of headaches and his health began to deteriorate rapidly. Nicholas had spent most of his time in London, away from Overlea Manor, but he'd witnessed his father's strange moods and increasing surliness on several occasions. Had witnessed how his father had pushed away all who'd loved him before the accident that had taken both of his parents' lives.

He remembered, too, how his older brother had developed the same mysterious ailment last year. An ailment that had led to his death.

His father had been sixty when he'd first started complaining about headaches. His brother's attacks had started much earlier, at the age of thirty-two, and his illness had progressed more quickly. Nicholas was only twenty-eight, but he could no longer ignore the fact he was now showing signs of suffering from that same disease.

Pushing back his grim thoughts, he opened his eyes and squinted against the bright light streaming through the window. He began to sit up but froze when he took in the unfamiliar surroundings.

Vague images filtered back to him, most of them featuring a blond-haired, gray-eyed woman hovering over him. He frowned, trying to remember what had happened the night before, but his memory eluded him.

He surveyed the room around him. Where was he? Not in his London townhouse. He remembered receiving a letter from his grandmother the day before. While not unusual, his grandmother's letters were rare enough to make him wary since she never bothered him with good news.

He closed his eyes and concentrated on the memory. He'd arrived home yesterday afternoon, and a footman had presented him with the letter. He remembered wondering what bad news he was about to read as he proceeded to his study and threw the letter on the desk. He'd poured himself a brandy before picking up the letter again and breaking the seal.

And that was all. Try as he might, he couldn't remember what his grandmother had written. Nor could he remember anything after that. He must have read the letter. He always did. He'd learned long ago there was no point in putting off bad news.

He opened his eyes at the sound of the door opening to find a woman standing there. Could this be the woman he remembered hovering over him last night? She was younger than he'd thought— not yet twenty if his guess was correct. Her long blond hair, tousled from sleep, trailed over her shoulders.

He frowned. Had he spent the night with her? He must have been truly out of his head, because he didn't usually dally with girls who were barely out of the schoolroom.

She was rubbing the sleep from her eyes when she entered. When her gaze met his, she froze. Her eyes were blue and wide with shock. Then, to his surprise, she opened her mouth and screamed.

Well, this was different. He'd made many women shriek in his day, but usually with pleasure.

BOOKS BY SUZANNA MEDEIROS

Dear Stranger

Forbidden in February (A Year Without a Duke multi-author series)

Anthologies:

The Novellas: A Collection

Hathaway Heirs: Books 1-4

Landing a Lord: Books 1-3

Landing a Lord series:

Dancing with the Duke

Loving the Marquess

Beguiling the Earl

The Unaffected Earl

The Unsuitable Duke

The Unexpected Marquess

The Unwilling Viscount (Coming in 2022)

Christmas Scandals series:

A Viscount for Christmas

A Highwayman for Christmas (Christmas 2022)

Hathaway Heirs series:

Lady Hathaway's Proposal

Lord Hathaway's Bride

Captain Hathaway's Dilemma

Miss Hathaway's Wish

For more information please visit the author's website:

https://www.suzannamedeiros.com/books/

USA Today bestselling author Suzanna Medeiros was born and raised in Toronto, Canada. Her love for the written word led her to pursue a degree in English Literature from the University of Toronto. She went on to earn a Bachelor of Education degree but graduated at a time when no teaching jobs were available. After working at a number of interesting places, including a federal inquiry, a youth probation office, and the Office of the Fire Marshal of Ontario, she decided to pursue her first love—writing.

Suzanna is married to her own hero and is the proud mother of twin daughters. She is an avowed romantic who enjoys spending her days writing love stories.

She would like to thank her parents for showing her that love at first sight and happily ever after really do exist.

To learn about Suzanna Medeiros's future books (and to receive a bonus short story!) sign up for her newsletter:
https://www.suzannamedeiros.com/newsletter

Visit her website:
https://www.suzannamedeiros.com

Or visit her on Facebook:
https://www.facebook.com/
AuthorSuzannaMedeiros